OLIVER CRUM AND THE BRIARWOOD WITCH

OLIVER CRUM BOOK 1

CHRIS COOPER

DREADFUL MEDIA

Oliver Crum and the Briarwood Witch

Published by Dreadful Media

Enjoy the book? Please consider leaving a review at goodreads.com or amazon.com. Every review helps. To receive news of new publications, events, and exclusive offers, please sign up for the Dreadful Media Newsletter on our website.
WWW.DREADFULMEDIA.COM

SPECIAL THANKS

Benjamin D. Smith
Emerson Kasak
Pete & Ro Maurer
Petra Gisela Sørensen

CHAPTER ONE

Ticktock.

The grandfather clock stood at the front of the room as a solemn reminder the workday was less than halfway done.

Ticktock.

The large metal pendulum swung back and forth, taunting him with the promise of another passing second.

Ticktock.

The rhythm pulsed behind his eyes.

Oliver hated the clock—no, he loathed the clock. The ticking wooden tower was a symbol of his perpetual servitude. He had resigned himself to sitting in his cubicle for eight hours a day until his life fell away and he became nothing more than an old bag of bones.

Tick.

A crash came from the other side of the room and pulled Oliver out of his existential crisis. Maurice had flipped over in his desk chair and was lying on the floor, clutching his chest. The man was in his midfifties, smoked like a chimney, and now found himself in the throes of a massive heart attack.

Several employees gathered around him, unsure of how to help, while the receptionist called 911. An intern pushed through the crowd, holding a white bottle of some sort, and knelt down next to him. She twisted off the cap and put a tablet into Maurice's mouth.

"Chew!" she yelled.

But Maurice couldn't chew. In fact, Maurice couldn't do anything, wouldn't do anything ever again, aside from stare vacantly up at the ceiling. The intern backed away from the lump of peach flesh protruding from a tangle of dark-gray suit, and for a moment, Oliver felt as if the air had been sucked out of the room. The cluster of coworkers stood in shock.

After fifteen agonizing minutes, the ambulance finally arrived, and the entire office staff shuffled outside to the parking lot to watch the paramedics cart Maurice away. The edges of the pale-blue cloth draped over the man's body fluttered in the cool breeze.

"Do you believe it? Just like that." Tony snapped his fingers, drawing a few glares from those around him. "Dead!"

Oliver believed it because he'd seen it happen. The poor guy had keeled over while answering an e-mail. *An e-mail—of all the pointless things!* The message was still on Maurice's screen when he crashed to the floor— something about an incorrect invoice number.

"Think they'd let me have his chair?" Tony asked, interrupting Oliver's train of thought. "It's one of those with the lumbar support lever, and my back's been *killing* me." He chuckled at his ill-timed joke while the others around him groaned.

Oliver clenched a fist. He shot a spiteful glance in Tony's direction and felt the onset of indigestion burbling up his esophagus. He swallowed hard, trying to squelch the burn.

"All right, all right, everybody back to work. And if you didn't clock out before coming out here, I expect you to take it out of your lunch time today." Mr. Sally held his arms out to his sides and gestured for everyone to go back inside. Oliver's boss was a solid foot shorter than he but had a temper to make up for his stature. The man was all about the bottom line, and not even an employee's death would give him pause if it meant lost productivity.

The office quickly returned to normal, but the white noise of the ringing phones and shuffling paper couldn't drown out the thoughts swirling in Oliver's head. *How can everyone just go back to work as if nothing happened?* He did his best to finish the engineering drawing he'd been working on but caught himself staring repeatedly at the empty cube across the aisle. A smattering of framed photographs sat on Maurice's desk, images of family picnics, birthdays, and graduations. Office policy restricted how employees could decorate their cubes, but Maurice had still managed to fill his with reminders of why he showed up to work every day. *Who would tell his family?* Oliver winced at the thought. *Surely not Mr. Sally.*

After several minutes of staring at the blinking cursor on his screen, Oliver walked to the break room for a cup of coffee, hoping to clear his mental fog. As he opened the door, he heard someone sniffling on the other side. Jeanine, the office secretary, quickly tried to compose herself.

"Are you all right?" he asked, sitting across the table from her.

"Oh, sorry. I'm fine," she said, balling up a tissue and concealing it in her sweater sleeve. Her horn-rimmed frames had fallen to the tip of her nose, and she slid them back into place with an index finger. "Maurice started here the same year I did. We worked together for nearly thir—"

The break room door swung open.

"The phone's ringing off the hook out there. Do I have to answer it myself?" Mr. Sally asked.

"I'm so sorry, sir. I was just on my way back." She snorted and shuffled to gather her things.

Mr. Sally looked at Oliver. "And shouldn't you be on your way too?"

Oliver avoided eye contact. "On my way," he affirmed, slipping out of the chair and heading toward the door. *What a slimeball.*

The train ride home was packed, and Oliver felt like a sardine crammed in a metal tin with a hundred other strangers. Fortunately, his height allowed him to stick his head out above the crowd, and his hair caught the subtle breeze from the train vents oscillating above him. He wondered where all the passengers were headed. *Are they all returning from their menial jobs to tiny cookie-cutter apartments like mine?*

"Don't be so dramatic," he said under his breath, drawing a sympathetic smile from the woman sitting next to him.

"Drury Street." The barely intelligible words spurted from the PA system.

The crowd swelled toward the door as the shuffling masses tried to squeeze between stationary passengers clinging tightly to metal poles and hand grips, trying hard not to be carried away by the mob. Oliver spotted a narrow pathway and sidestepped out of the train. The clomp of hundreds of shoes against the subway tile created a hum that echoed through the station. The pull of the crowd carried him up the stairs, where it spilled out onto the city sidewalk and quickly dispersed.

Oliver's studio apartment was located in a dreary stone high-rise, which blended into its stormy-sky back-drop. He entered through the revolving door just as rain began to fall. He dried his feet on the forest-green carpet and checked his small mailbox. The once-lavish lobby had fallen into disrepair after the owner had sold the building to developers who subdivided a large chunk of the luxury apartments into studios. Oliver hadn't seen them, but one of the maintenance guys mentioned the owners had even split two floors into microapartments—basically hallways just large enough to fit a few belongings and a bed. He was fortunate enough to afford the studio although that might not be the case for much longer if rent continued to climb.

Although the building contained two elevators, the one that went to the lower levels had been out of order for weeks. Five flights of stairs stood between Oliver and his small studio, and the climb seemed longer and longer every time. When he reached the fifth floor, he fumbled for his keychain, which had become tangled in his headphones. He slid the key into the deadbolt and had to practically break the key off in the tumblers to get it to open. The landlord had promised to fix the lock months before and was now no longer responding to Oliver's phone calls. He was greeted by a butterscotch tabby who brushed her coat against the hem of his pants, leaving a trail of orange behind. Nekko was a whale of a cat, and Oliver found it hard to believe he had once been able to hold her in the palm of his hand.

He set his messenger bag on a small writing desk underneath the only window in the apartment and pulled up a chair. The city skyline disappeared into the mist although he could clearly make out the cars on the bustling street below. For the most part, the city had been good to him. He had been lucky enough to land a job right after graduation, and at twenty-four years old, Oliver had all the consistency and comfort one could ever desire. A local bookstore sat one block down from his complex, and he frequented the Chinese restaurant directly across the street. If he was lucky, he could make it all the way down to dinner and back without having to speak to a soul, aside from the hostess at the restaurant. He liked her. One day, while waiting for his sweet-and-sour chicken, she mentioned she'd been a doctor in China. Oliver wasn't exactly sure of a career plan that led to a Chinese doctor working as a hostess, but he enjoyed talking to her all the same.

Movies stacked the wall next to Oliver's bed. Countless disc cases and a stack of VHS tapes were arranged in alphabetical order. At precisely nine p.m. every night, Oliver chose a movie from the collection and passed out in front of the fluorescent glow of his small TV. The routine wasn't thrilling, but he had come to depend on it as a way of providing a momentary escape to another world that offered a bit more mystery and adventure. He specialized in horror films but watched everything from Ingmar Bergman to Woody Allen. The walls of the apartment were even lined with old sketches from some of his favorite movies.

During his first few months at the firm, Oliver would occasionally will himself down to the art-supply store after work to buy a poster board and sketch a life-size character for his wall. The boards started to form a mural of sorts, and he'd even begun to tie the pieces together with decorative filigree. At first, sketching had provided him with a creative outlet, but he stopped altogether when the job became too tiring. The drawing of Vincent Price seemed to look upon him with a glint of judgment in his eye every time Oliver passed the neglected sketchbooks on his way to the TV.

Oliver slid his worn copy of *The Devil's Backbone* into the VHS player and settled into bed with the cat curled up next to him.

CHAPTER TWO

The beige ceiling tiles slowly came into focus as Oliver lay on his back on the cheap frayed carpet of his cubicle.

"Take him out back," Mr. Sally said, leaning over him, his bulbous nose pulsing red. He snapped his fingers at Tony and gestured for him to take Oliver away.

"I'm fine," Oliver replied. "I just need a little help getting up. I must have slipped."

"No, no," his boss corrected him. "You're dead." Mr. Sally motioned again.

Oliver could feel himself being dragged. He tried to wrench himself free from Tony's grip, but some invisible force fused his limbs in place, preventing him from fighting back. The cement scraped against his backside as Tony pulled him outside and over to the old dumpster. Wispy clouds filled the blue sky above him, and he stared upward, trying to identify the fluffy patterns and momentarily forgetting his predicament. With one great heave, Tony somehow managed to lift Oliver into the dumpster, and the bright sky was consumed by darkness.

Oliver held on to the last fleeting moments of sleep as Nekko walked on his small intestine. The cat, growing impatient with his lack of response, began to knead his bladder.

"All right, all right! I get the point. I'm getting up," he said, swatting the cat off him.

As he rolled over, his entire body ached with exhaustion. The paranoid nightmare was the cherry on top of his sleepless-night sundae. Still, the dream must have been his mind's way of dealing with the thought that had been nagging him—he couldn't let himself meet a similar fate as Maurice. He was miserable, and something had to change.

Oliver took a deep breath. "You're being dramatic," he said aloud. "Millions of people have it way worse than you do. Get over yourself." The affirmation seemed to calm his nerves, and he rolled onto his side to check the time.

The flashing screen of the alarm clock greeted him. *The power must have gone out again.* His grogginess evaporated immediately, replaced by dread, and he reached for his watch. *I'm late!*

Oliver rolled out of bed and ran to the bathroom to ready himself for the day. The heavy thuds against the bathroom door indicated Nekko's breakfast time was long past.

His dress shirt flapped in the wind as he rushed down the stairs and onto the platform of the train station. Tony had been late a few weeks before, and Mr. Sally chewed him out in front of the entire office. Oliver's cheeks flushed at the thought of his boss's chubby finger wagging in his face. In the midst of his imagined predicament, he missed his subway stop. *It's official. I'm dead.* He had no time to wait for the train back, so he decided to run the last few blocks to work.

Although he tried to regain composure before walking into the office lobby, his tie was tied approximately three inches too short, and his dress shirt was drenched with sweat. Jeanine looked up from her desk and gave him a grim "good morning." If he kept his head down, he might just be able to slip in without being noticed. He sneaked down the hallway and around the corner into the cube farm. The boss's office had a large picture window overlooking the floor, but fortunately, Mr. Sally was preoccupied with a phone call. Oliver power walked to his cubicle and set his bag down. He turned to look at his boss once more, caught the corner of Mr. Sally's gaze, and ducked into his cubicle to wait for the threat to pass. After a few tense seconds, he peeked his head out over the cube wall. This time, his boss was standing on the other side of the glass, staring directly at him.

The sound of Mr. Sally's Italian loafers shuffling against the carpet filled Oliver's heart with dread. He didn't bother to sit back down—sitting would have done no good. He simply stood and watched his boss approach, finger pointed in his direction.

"How dare you!" Mr. Sally said. Oliver had been right about the finger wag.

"Sir, I'm—" he started.

"No!" his boss yelled. "I don't want to hear your excuses. You're an adult, aren't you?"

He said nothing, but his boss waited for a response.

"I asked you a question," he said.

"I..." Oliver was petrified and couldn't get the words to leave his lips.

"Being an adult means that you show up on time. You are an adult, aren't you?"

Spittle flew from his boss's lips and speckled Oliver's cheeks. He wanted to wipe it away but dared not move.

"Now Maurice is out of the picture, we'll all have to pick up the slack. His replacement won't be here for another week at the earliest, and we don't have time to goof off in the meantime."

Oliver glanced at Maurice's cube, or at least what had been Maurice's cube. The pictures and personal items had been removed, and all that remained was an empty desk. Tony must have taken the office chair. The man's entire existence at the company had been wiped away in a single morning.

"Are you even listening to me?" His boss's voice was becoming raspy from all the yelling. "I think Maurice would still be more competent than you."

The last line caught Oliver's attention. He stared down at the squat man glaring up at him. Mr. Sally's forehead was flush with anger, and his nose was lined with thin red varicose veins from years of afternoon scotches. Maybe Oliver was shell-shocked from Maurice's death or perhaps just delirious from the lack of sleep followed by the pavement-pounding dash to work, but something in him snapped. At that moment, everything else faded away except for Mr. Sally's voice, punctuated by the staccato notes of the ticking grandfather clock.

Tick.

"Am I talking to myself?"

Tock.

"I ought to fire you right—"

Tick.

"Then do it!" Oliver yelled with such sudden force it knocked his boss backward several paces.

"Excuse me?" Mr. Sally replied.

"Here, I'll make it easy for you." Oliver marched toward the front of the room as heads slowly popped out from behind cubicle walls.

Even Tony, who had been enjoying his newly acquired office chair, stood up to watch the events unfold.

The grandfather clock was a company heirloom and had come to represent everything Oliver hated about the place. The constant ticking reminded him that life was slowly but surely slipping away.

The next few moments were fuzzy, but when Oliver came to, he was standing in front of the room, towering over the overturned clock. Shards of glass lay scattered on the floor, and everyone in the cube farm was staring at him. Not a soul moved, and the white noise of shuffling papers and phone conversations had stopped completely. His boss, who was never speechless, stood frozen in place, mouth gaping wide.

Oliver's uncharacteristic rage was quickly replaced by utter panic. A white-hot heat filled his cheeks, and his body tingled with embarrassment. Without saying another word, he sprinted from the room, past the reception desk, and out the front door.

What have I done? What have I done? The thought

looped in Oliver's mind. After the incident at the office, he ran from the building toward the train station, discarding his tie in a trash can along the way. Just that morning, he had sprinted in the opposite direction, trying to pull himself together, but now he shed bits of his office uniform like an old car shedding parts.

The train ride home was painfully long, and he spent the majority of the journey trying to figure out how to undo the mess he had made. But he couldn't just turn around, and surely his boss was already filling out the termination paperwork. This couldn't be undone, and the realization was both terrifying and liberating. He had wanted a change. *But how could I have been so careless? What do I do now?* He had no backup plan, no other job waiting in the wings. In one sweeping motion, he had brought the old grandfather clock crashing down on his future. He scanned his brain for options. He couldn't go back home to his mother—she wouldn't understand and probably wouldn't let him in the door if he told her. He could think of only one place that was safe—a place where he could clear his head and get his life back in order—and that place was far from the city.

The maintenance man's toolbox sat outside the broken lobby elevator. A hand emerged from the car and fished around in the toolbox until it emerged holding a screwdriver. Oliver found it ironic the landlord had finally decided to have the elevator fixed on the day of his great escape.

The frayed carpet had begun to pull loose from the wooden staircase, and the tacks caught the tips of his rubber soles as he climbed. He laughed. *Everything about this place seems to be holding me back.*

Two duffel bags. He fit all the critical pieces of his life into two duffel bags, and one of them was devoted solely to his obese butterscotch tabby. A cat carrier was a luxury he couldn't afford, so he lined one of the bags with a few soft towels and coaxed the cat inside. While most cats would have gone crazy if confined to a bag, Nekko simply turned around a few times and plopped herself down onto the soft makeshift bed. He zipped the bag closed three-quarters of the way, leaving enough space for her head. The other duffel was crammed with a few sets of clothes and one or two of Oliver's most sentimental mementos. The rest could stay behind for the time being.

His savings account held enough cash to cover rent for the next few months, which would give him enough time to sort his life out and find a new job. But for now, he needed a momentary reprieve from the city and all the stresses that came along with it.

After buying a train ticket at the station window, he settled in on a wooden bench to wait for the next train. One of his duffel bags slowly rose and fell next to him, a sign his feline companion was fast asleep inside. He stuck his finger into the unzipped portion of the bag and scratched under Nekko's chin. Her purr was too soft to hear over the ambient noise of the station, but he could feel the vibration through his fingertip.

Oliver traced the subway tiles with his eyes, following the lines of black grout along the wall leading to the Drury Street sign. When the train arrived, he took one last look at the station before stepping inside. Something about the ebb and flow of the crowd was soothing. He found relief in blending in with the sea of people and, at the same time, a sense of belonging to something larger than himself.

CHAPTER THREE

The scenery flew by as the stark urban landscape gradually transformed into lush green fields and rocky hillsides.

Oliver sipped the tea he'd purchased from the snack trolley and tried to calm his nerves. His eyes followed the wavy line of wooden fences whizzing by, and he counted horses and cows dotting the passing farmland in sporadic patches.

He could think of only one place to go—a house in a little town at the edge of the woods.

"Ticket please," the conductor said, reaching out a white-gloved hand. Oliver shuffled through his pockets and produced a small slip of paper, which the man stamped and handed back to him.

"Know how much longer it'll be?" Oliver asked.

The conductor tugged a chain that disappeared

into his front pants pocket, revealing an elaborate golden pocket watch on the other end. He flipped the cover open and glanced at the watch face. "Oh, I'd say another forty-five minutes or so." He closed the watch and tucked it away.

Oliver's thoughts were punctuated with worry, and despite his best efforts to rid his mind of panic, he couldn't help but think in worst-case scenarios. He was still unsure of exactly what would happen from that point forward. His decision to pack had been a split-second one, and he had planned only up to the point of boarding the train. Spontaneity wasn't normally in his nature. *What if she doesn't want me to stay?*

The train lurched to a halt as it pulled up to the platform, and Oliver gathered his things and walked toward the sliding exit door. The station was a modest one, and few exited the train with him. The place hadn't changed a bit since he'd last been there, more than a decade before. In fact, he immediately recognized the small candy store across the tracks. The red-and-white stripes on the awning had faded a bit, but the walls of the store were still lined with jars of colorful confections. Compared to the dinginess of the city station, Christchurch Station was pristine. The tile floors had been scrubbed to a pearly luminescence, and the walls were free of the layers of haphazardly taped flyers that plastered those in the city. A station attendant chased a rogue piece of plastic wrapper that skittered across the platform.

Oliver lugged the two duffel bags—one much heavier than the other—over to the town map. If he recalled correctly, the house was through the square and down the dirt road next to the market, but he couldn't remember where exactly the market was located.

The large Welcome to Christchurch sign greeted him as he left the station. The town square was still paved with bricks that must have been more than a century old. He could feel the unevenness under his feet and occasionally caught the tips of his shoes on their edges as he walked. An imposing bronze statue of the town founder stood in the center of the square. Like the pristine tiles in the station, the bronze had been polished to an impeccable shine. As a kid, Oliver had been creeped out by the statue, which had towered over his boyish frame. Now, the figure appeared almost comical. A pious caricature of the town founder stood bearing a large cross and reaching up toward the heavens. The eyes still appeared to follow him, though, as he approached the bronze plaque that summarized the founding of Christchurch. A small group of settlers, fleeing from religious persecution, had set up camp there several hundred years before and never left. He hadn't noticed before, but a small bronze seal had been engraved in the top corner of the plaque. A limp serpent hung from the top of a cross, its body twisted around the cross's base. The symbol reminded Oliver of something he'd seen on the side of a hospital, two serpents twisted around a staff with a set of angelic wings perched at the top. This symbol was different, though.

Nekko grew heavy on Oliver's shoulder, and the duffel strap dug into his collarbone. The short walk to the station was nothing compared to the walk across town, and he tried to alleviate the shoulder pain by repositioning the strap of the bag with no luck.

"You're going on a diet," he said, looking down at the small patch of orange peeking through the open zipper.

He passed a row of stores, most of which had already closed for the day. As the sun set on the town, it aligned perfectly with the peak of the town hall, creating a beautiful silhouette surrounded by a warm orange glow. The square itself seemed to be stuck in another time. The buildings were understated, with designs and colors that ensured no one building stood out from the others, except for the bakery on the right side of the square. The shop's brilliant colors and decorations screamed for his attention. He was happy to see *she* hadn't changed much since his last visit.

Oliver made it to the market and turned left down

an ill-defined dirt road. In another half mile, he would arrive at the house, and he just hoped someone was home. Not many people lived down that way. Most lived on the left or right of the square, tucked into the small grid-shaped blocks that patterned the country-side behind the shops. No, this side of the square led to the forest, and few lived near the forest. Based on the mostly undisturbed dirt beneath his feet, not many even ventured this way.

The three-story house stood at the top of a valley, overlooking the field sitting adjacent to the forest. The home's bright-yellow siding had faded a bit since his last visit, but the place was still an oasis compared to its uninhabited surroundings. As Oliver walked toward the stairs of the curved wraparound porch, he looked up at the large turret above him. The house was completely dark except for a single light coming from the curved window. *She's home!*

He pressed a finger on the cracked plastic of the doorbell, but the chime must have been broken. Oliver rapped his knuckle on the wooden storm door, and a distant bark echoed through the house. *Clearly, she doesn't need a doorbell.* The bark wasn't the type that would keep intruders at bay, more of a playful puppy yip. After a few moments, he heard the scurry of little nails against the hardwood floor, and the front porch light burst to life.

The door opened just enough to reveal the slender nose of the old woman on the other side.

"Who is it?" she asked.

"It's me. Oliver," he replied.

The security chain rattled loose, and the woman's colorful frame came into view as she opened the door. She had long gray hair and red spectacles and wore a colorful muumuu, which seemed to swallow her delicate frame.

"What are you doing here?" she asked, throwing her arms around him.

The force of her hug caused him to stumble backward, and he put a foot back to brace himself.

"How long has it been?" she asked. "Is everything okay?" Her expression shifted from one of happiness to concern. "Is your mom okay?"

"Yeah, everything's fine," he lied. "Mind if I come in and set this stuff down? Sorry to barge in on you like this."

"Of course. Come in, come in. Just watch out for Pan. He has a bad habit of getting under people's feet," she replied.

Sure enough, as he stepped over the threshold, the small corgi pup weaved in and out between his legs.

To say Oliver's aunt Izzy had eclectic tastes would have been an understatement. Her living room was filled with neon-colored furniture and obscure artwork, most of her own design. A stack of canvases sat in the corner of the room, and the shelves were lined with knickknacks and mementos scattered haphazardly between miniature sculptures made from junk. Compared to Oliver's drab fifth-floor studio, this place was bursting at the seams with character.

Izzy led him to the kitchen, where she filled a kettle of water to boil. He set his duffel bags underneath the kitchen table, which roused Nekko from her deep slumber. Pan was quick to notice the shuffling bag and poked his snout through the unzipped portion. A deep growl emerged from inside, and a large butterscotch paw appeared from the opening and slapped the dog across the nose. The surprise attack sent Pan leaping backward, at least as far as a pup with inch-long legs could leap.

Izzy stirred a spoonful of honey into her tea although she struggled to grip the small teaspoon. Her fingers had started to bend unnaturally with age, a sign of the slow creep of arthritis. Oliver referred to Izzy as his aunt even though she was actually his great aunt. He'd called her that once too, but the harsh reprimand that followed deterred him from doing so again. She owned the oddly decorated town bakery he'd passed on the way in. The Rolling Pin also kept the town in fresh supply of honey from the bees Izzy raised in the backyard.

Oliver took a swig from his teacup and placed it on the kitchen table, which had been fashioned out of an old industrial cable spool, painted a bright aqua, and embellished with intricate floral designs.

"So, you just got up and left?" she asked.

"Well, not exactly. First, I destroyed a company heirloom in a fit of rage," he replied.

Izzy perked up in her chair.

Though the clock assassination was still a blur, he could feel an anxious knot forming in his stomach as he told the pieces of the story he could remember. "I can't believe I did it. I mean, I didn't like my job, but still... I just threw everything away. I feel terrible."

Izzy looked up at Oliver. "You don't seem like a person to do something so brazen without a reason. I've been arrested for my fair share of transgressions, mostly protest related, and there was the time I stole that miniature horse, but you're a rule follower. What got into you?" She wasn't scolding him but rather asking out of general curiosity.

"I don't know," Oliver replied. "I just couldn't take it anymore." He leaned over and pressed his forehead against the table.

"Perhaps you were just giving yourself an ultimatum, forcing your hand. You were miserable and couldn't let yourself continue to live that way." Izzy looked down at her hands for a moment, as if debating whether or not to speak. "Have you told your mom?"

The question caught Oliver off guard, and his stomach gurgled at the thought. As far as he knew, Izzy hadn't spoken to his mother in years, since their falling out after his grandmother's death.

"She doesn't need to know. I'll find another job and just tell her I'm leaving the old one to pursue it."

"Well, what's done is done," Izzy said after an uncomfortable moment of silence, "and all you can do now is move forward. I'm glad you're here. You ought to stay for a few weeks while you get back on your feet." She reached across the table and placed her hand on his head. "It's going to be fine."

Although he appreciated Izzy's kindness, Oliver was certain things wouldn't be *"fine." How could they be?* Not only was he going to lose his job, but his boss's tentacles ran deep in the local business community—he'd be lucky if he could find a job flipping burgers. At least no one in Christchurch, aside from Izzy, knew who he was or what he had done.

CHAPTER FOUR

Oliver lay on his back, head floating somewhere between the dreaming and the waking world. Just as the haze of sleep started to fade, a bright beam of light burst from the window. As he put a hand to his forehead to shield his eyes, he noticed an alien lifeform opening the curtains. He jumped from the bed and onto his feet.

"About time you're up," the creature said.

"What do you want?" he slurred, still not fully awake.

The being raised its hands and removed its helmet, revealing the face of a harmless old woman underneath. Izzy stood there in full beekeeper uniform.

"You've been in bed all day. I know you're stressed, but this isn't going to help." She shook a finger at Oliver, her hand covered with a white beekeeper's glove. "Come on. I'm going to the bakery, and you're going to help me. You need some sunlight and a little social interaction." Her voice was about as serious as he'd ever heard it. She'd never had any kids and hadn't developed the stern motherly voice that often accompanied a scolding and the use of a middle name. Still, he obliged.

While Izzy went to change, Oliver yanked an old pair of sweatpants and a college sweatshirt from his duffel bag and slipped them on. He sat slumped over on the bed, trying to wipe the sleep from his eyes and wishing he could crawl back under the covers and doze for another week.

"Come on! Come on!" Izzy yelled from the other room.

Oliver slogged downstairs and slid on a pair of gym shoes.

She led him out the front door by the arm and turned to go back inside. "You get in the car. I've got to grab a few boxes from the kitchen."

The robin-egg-blue station wagon sat beneath the porte cochere. Izzy had taken him around in the car as a child, and it had become the Rolling Pin's official delivery car when she bought the bakery a few years back. Sure, most of its parts had been replaced over the years, but its heart remained the same, at least according to Izzy.

The tan leather seat seared Oliver's skin, and he pulled down his shirt to cover any remaining bits of exposed flesh. The sensation brought back memories of his last visit, shortly after his tenth birthday. He'd stayed with Izzy while his parents dealt with something his mom referred to as a 'rough patch.' He didn't realize until much later how close they'd been to divorce.

Izzy bounced the screen door open with her elbow and emerged from the house, holding a stack of cardboard boxes.

"Need some help?" he yelled from the car as he started to open the door.

"I got it. I may be old, but I can still lift a few boxes," she replied. After loading the cargo into the back of the car, she climbed into the driver's seat.

"What's in the boxes?" he asked.

"Honey for the store. We're running low."

The town was alive and bustling, in stark contrast to the subdued village Oliver had stumbled through the previous night. The car turned left at the market, which had an array of brightly colored fruits on display in wooden barrels out front. Two elderly women sorted through piles of oranges, squeezing them one by one, checking for freshness. The Rolling Pin sat on the other side of the town, next to a small law office. Izzy pulled the car around back, to the service entrance, and

Oliver helped carry the boxes inside. The building had once been an abandoned lodge used for town celebrations, church, and club meetings. The town quickly outgrew the structure and built a larger hall on the other side of the square. The move left the original building vacant and in need of a new purpose, and Izzy was happy to oblige. Oliver had only seen the bakery in pictures prior to this visit, and the place was even more whimsical in person.

The Rolling Pin had all the traditional markings of a bakery but was also speckled with colorful bits and bobs that reflected Izzy's vibrant personality. The entire front of the building was covered in chalk drawings, and she left a tub of sidewalk chalk out front so the neighborhood kids could draw whatever they pleased. Her collection of lawn gnomes stood guard over the front door, as did a giant metal dragon sculpture made from recycled pipes, gears, and bicycle chains. The bakery was unlike any Oliver had ever seen and was out of place amidst the town's historic aesthetic.

The interior of the bakery was no less flashy. The dark-green display cases rose to Oliver's chest and were filled with rows upon rows of tempting baked goods. He walked past cupcakes made to look like potted plants and admired the intricately decorated sugar cookies, which were topped with delicately piped honeybees. The displays were arranged in a U shape that formed an archipelago to the kitchen. Chrome industrial mixers and other kitchen gadgetry peeked out from behind the open doorway.

The bakery not only housed tons of baked goods but also dealt in crafts and local artwork. Several hand-stitched quilts hung from racks along the walls, and a set of copper fountains sat for sale next to a row of dining booths. The booths themselves were hand-painted, with deep-red vinyl cushions. A collection of Izzy's paintings hung around the room, and a few of her smaller sculptures sat on the booth tables. The bakery was truly unique, and the hundreds of tiny touches here and there would have made it impossible to replicate.

Only one thing was missing from the store—people. The place was vacant, with no customers in sight. Oliver found this odd, since it was midmorning, and he assumed bakeries did most of their business in the mornings. *Coffee and donuts. That's a thing, right?*

"You can put the boxes in the back," she said. "I'm going to check the mail."

"What time do you open?" Oliver asked.

"We opened hours ago," she replied, walking toward the door.

He set the boxes on one of the display cases so he could lift the hinged counter to the back. Although the kitchen was mostly hidden from view of the customers, it had just as much artistic flare as the front of the house. The walls were covered with bright-yellow tiles, and an intricate mosaic patterned one of the walls. The design reminded Oliver of a Celtic tree of life, which protected those shaded by it and provided them with food and shelter. The branches intertwined, covered with little green leaves made from bits of chipped tile. He stood immersed in its beauty, completely forgetting that the boxes were, in fact, fairly heavy.

"Can I help you?" someone said from behind, nearly making him drop the boxes of fragile jars.

"Just dropping off a few boxes of honey," he replied, turning to face the mystery woman. "Izzy's my great aunt."

The woman stood on the other side of a large metal table. She brushed a patch of flour from her face and wiped her hands on her apron.

"You must be Oliver, then. Izzy mentioned you might be stopping over. Nice to meet you," she said, reaching to shake his hand. "I'm Anna."

Her handshake was incredibly firm, and he winced a bit when she gripped his hand.

"Oh, sorry about that," she said, lightening up on her grip. "The years of kneading dough have done wonders for my forearms." Anna's strawberry-blond hair caught the sunlight when she laughed, hinting at her Irish roots, as did her slightly freckled face. "So, how long are you here for, then?"

"Maybe a few weeks or so. Not really sure, to be honest," he replied. He had momentarily forgotten about his current predicament, but her question brought his past crashing back into him. He swallowed hard to squelch the wave of nausea.

Anna seemed to sense his discomfort. "Why don't you take those down to the cellar and put them on the rack next to the others? The door's right over there."

Oliver carried the boxes over to the door but couldn't manage to turn the knob. Anna, seeing his struggle, rushed over to open it for him.

"And watch the pipe," she said, ushering him inside.

Oliver had to duck to avoid smacking his forehead on a large metal water pipe. The stairs were narrow, only as deep as the heel of his shoe, and he had to turn sideways to step comfortably. The old wooden boards creaked under his feet, and the steps must have been old enough to precede any building codes that would have made them safer to use.

The stones making up the basement floor had shifted over time, leaving an uneven surface with several hills and valleys. The metal storage racks sat at the far end of the cellar, their modern design juxta-posed against the aging stone foundation. He unboxed the honey and lined the jars neatly on the shelves. As he turned toward the staircase, he noticed something strange. Each of the wooden ceiling beams had the same pattern burned into it. Oliver grabbed an old folding chair from the corner of the room and stood on it to get a closer look. The symbol was the same as the one he'd found on the monument in the town square— the familiar snake draped over an old wooden cross.

"Find everything all right?" Anna asked while putting dough balls on the shelf to prove as Oliver emerged from the doorway.

"I did," Oliver replied. "The snake symbol on the wood beams downstairs—what does it mean? I saw the same thing on the plaque in the square."

Anna gave him a puzzled look. "Oh, that's the Elders' seal. They're kind of like a homeowner's association for the town. They have a lot of say over what happens around here and advise the mayor on new regulations and guidelines. Used to have a lot more power actually, but now they're basically just a group of influential old people who complain when someone hangs curtains that are too bright or puts out a 'distasteful' lawn decoration."

"They must love Izzy," he replied.

"They're also the reason why the shop is empty right now," she added. "She's on the agenda for the town meeting tonight, actually. They've been pressuring her to take down the decorations out front and bring the store in line with others in the square. She isn't happy about it, if you can imagine. When she refused to redo the front, they passed a new ordinance, just to target the bakery. When the daily fine didn't work, they initiated an unofficial boycott of sorts. Fortunately, we've got enough fans to stay in business right now—they just aren't willing to be seen here. Believe it or not, we do most of our business through secret delivery these days."

Oliver found it hard to imagine a group of old people with nothing better to do than dictate town decorations and create arbitrary regulations. Then he thought about his last visit with Izzy and was fairly certain his family would have thrived in Christchurch, a place where people were kept in line by an evolutionary need to fit in. His mom had sent him to Izzy's with a legal pad full of rules, which Izzy quickly discarded. During his visit, he stayed up late, ate too much ice cream, watched inappropriately scary movies, and was returned to his mother with a pair of ripped jeans and a large knee scab. Although he had a blast, his mom was less enthused and promptly informed Izzy he'd never stay with her again, once Oliver disclosed the full details of his visit. He would receive birthday and holiday cards from Izzy and called her every now and then in college but was somewhat ashamed this was the first time he'd ventured to Christchurch to see her on his own.

"They're a pain in my side," Izzy said as she walked into the kitchen. "A little color never hurt anyone, but they're too concerned with maintaining 'order' to worry about putting an old woman out of business."

"That's why we're going to the meeting at the town hall tonight," Anna said.

"I'm going to give those self-righteous geezers a piece of my mind," Izzy said, shaking a fist. The revolutionary flame in her heart still appeared to be burning brightly. "You should come. It'll be a great way to meet the fine townsfolk." She smirked.

CHAPTER FIVE

The town hall sat in stark contrast to the small businesses surrounding it. The front of the imposing stone building was lined with tall pillars that supported an elaborate archway and clock.

When Oliver thought of town-hall meetings, his mind went to empty boardrooms with lots of vacant chairs, cold coffee, and a few attendees with nothing better to do than complain about Christmas decorations that had been left out for too long. This place, on the other hand, was packed. A large wooden desk sat elevated at the front of the room, facing the audience. The hall itself was dimly lit and contained row upon row of wooden chairs, all of which were occupied. A balcony overlooked the town council's bench, and it too was filled to the brim.

Izzy, Anna, and Oliver all stood against the wall at

the back of the room, looking diligently for vacant seats.

"Are these meetings always this crowded?" Oliver asked.

"We're getting close to the town's anniversary, so it's been busier than usual, but the people here take town governance pretty seriously," Anna replied.

"Fascists," Izzy added under her breath.

Oliver felt a bony shoulder slam into his arm, which was hanging over slightly into the doorway.

"Excuse you," the woman said as she strode up the aisle toward the front of the room.

"Who's that ray of sunshine?" he whispered to Anna, rubbing his arm.

"Madeline." Anna said the name as if she were gagging on it. "She's the reigning Elder president and one of the reasons why the shop is a ghost town."

Madeline had the frame of an aged supermodel. She was tall, thin, and clad in a tailored black business suit and white blouse. Her silver hair had been styled into submission, with perfectly constructed layers completing her executive look. She marched to the front of the room and took a seat on the right side of the council desk. After shuffling through a stack of papers, something in the first row of chairs caught her eye. She hopped up from her seat and motioned toward the back of the room with her clutch, bobbing her head with each gesture. Two teenagers stood up and slowly sulked to the back of the room while Madeline watched to ensure their full cooperation. They found a place next to Izzy, just close enough for Oliver to hear them mumbling their dissatisfaction.

The rest of the council members took their seats, and the meeting came to order.

"That hunk in the middle is the mayor," Izzy whispered to Oliver. The mayor appeared to be in his forties, with broad shoulders, a chiseled jaw, and sandy-blond hair.

"Let's get started," the mayor said. "For the first item on the agenda, we have a committee update on the Christchurch tricentennial celebration. Cynthia, please go right ahead."

A woman stood in the center of a row of chairs but was so short that seeing her was difficult.

"Things are moving along swimmingly. We are in need of additional volunteers for booth setup and teardown, though. Is anyone interested?" She looked around the room.

Madeline gave a sharp glance to one side of the room, and a few hands immediately shot up from the crowd.

She really does control this town.

The meeting dragged on for more than an hour, but the time finally came for new business. Izzy stepped out from the back of the room and walked up to the small podium facing the imposing council desk. The council members towered over her as if she had committed a capital offense and was pleading for mercy from a hopefully magnanimous jury. Izzy had always appeared to be an extremely confident person, but even she seemed to waver somewhat in the spotlight.

"Um, yes. Two weeks ago, the council issued an ordinance violation and fine to the bakery, and I've come to ask that it be lifted," she said with a forced pleasantness.

The mayor started to speak, but Madeline jumped in before he had the opportunity.

"So, you've addressed the issues, then?" she asked.

"No, but—"

"The businesses in the town square are all required to follow a set of visual guidelines. You know this, Isabelle."

"Actually, I voted against—"

"How you voted doesn't matter. The ordinance passed by a majority vote, and you, as a business owner in the square, are obligated to follow the rules. We've been over this again and again—the front of your store is completely out of line. We have the tricentennial next week, and visitors are coming from all over the state. They come to admire Christchurch's historic beauty and our rustic charm, something they won't be able to do if confronted with that atrocity of a storefront."

"Hold on," Izzy said, quickly shedding her polite demeanor.

"Remove the decorations, and we'll lift the fine. Now, please step aside, and let the next person speak."

As Izzy clenched her fist and prepared for verbal warfare, Anna's voice boomed from the back of the room. "Now, you wait just a minute," she said.

Oliver turned to look at her, shocked by the sudden outburst and catching only a brief glimpse of her beet-red face as she squeezed by him and into the aisle.

"The matter has been se—" Madeline didn't have the opportunity to finish her sentence.

"I don't care, you old bat!"

This resulted in an audible gasp from the crowd, and the two teenagers next to Oliver snickered.

"You walk around here with nothing better to do than starve our business and make up stupid rules to target us. You've nearly run us into the ground!"

"That's enough!" The mayor stood, and his voice thundered across the room. He didn't need a gavel to get Anna's attention although he probably would have slammed it on the table if he had one. The loud inter-jection stopped her in her tracks. "You will not stand there and name call. If you have an issue with the policy—"

"But, Dad!" she pleaded.

"No, this is not the way we do things around here. Now, step away from the podium, and return to your seat."

Oliver watched her, his mouth agape as she stomped down the aisle and out the door, slamming it behind her. *Her dad is the mayor?*

Izzy stood next to the podium, seemingly unsure of whether to laugh or cry.

This particular town meeting must have been the most entertaining in some time, because the council had difficulty bringing the crowd back to order. Madeline clenched the edge of the desk and appeared to be digging into the wood with her fingernails.

"Anything else we can do for you today?" she asked Izzy in a mock-cheery tone.

CHAPTER SIX

The brightly colored chalk ran down the side of the building and into a gray puddle on the sidewalk. Izzy couldn't stand to wash the drawings away, so she'd asked Oliver to do it for her. He swept the garden hose back and forth, slowly erasing the images the town's children had so carefully crafted.

"I can't believe they're making her do this," Anna said. "I'm so angry I still can't see straight. I've already started plotting my revenge, but the most sinister thing I could think of was to put too much vanilla in the tricentennial cake."

"Dastardly," he replied.

Unable to afford the continuing fines and dwindling customers, Izzy had agreed to restore order to the storefront. Upon her notification to the council, business rapidly returned to normal, and they had even asked Izzy to bake the town's celebration cake as a sign of goodwill.

"I told her to imagine there had been a bad thunderstorm. It's just chalk," Oliver said. "We could set the kids loose on the building, and it would be back to normal in an afternoon."

"That's not the point." Anna turned toward him with clenched fists at her side. "She shouldn't have to do this. She didn't do anything wrong and is just being punished for being different. They made the rule to target her."

"That's kind of how life works, isn't it?" The question slipped from Oliver's lips before he could catch it behind his teeth.

"What a miserable way to look at the world. I've got to get back inside. More orders to fill." She huffed.

He felt bad for being so cynical but didn't see the big deal—it was just the outside of the building. In college, his Japanese friend had once taught him an old saying: "The nail that sticks out gets hammered down." Oliver believed it, and clearly Christchurch believed it too. But the situation could have been much worse.

After spraying the walls clean, he brought the fleet of garden gnomes inside to keep watch over the bakery display cases. The dragon statue was too heavy for him to lift by himself, but he wanted to give Anna some time to cool off before asking for help. He knew she wasn't really angry with him, but he certainly hadn't made the situation any better.

The bakery was more crowded than Oliver had seen it. He assumed Izzy would be overjoyed with the turnout, but instead, she hid in the kitchen for most of the day. Anna had taken over the front of the store but struggled to keep everything under control by herself.

"Give me a hand with these orders," she said to Oliver. "Everything's on the receipt—just need to grab items from the cases and bag them up." She still had an edge to her voice but was drowning in customers and clearly needed a life preserver.

"Happy to help. Where's Izzy?" he asked, walking around to the other side of the counter.

"Think she's down for the count. Might want to go check on her after you help me," she replied, handing change to a customer.

He grabbed a set of tongs and assembled the carryout orders. Once the line died down, he went back into the kitchen to check on Izzy. She sat on a stool at the big kitchen table, clutching a cup of tea.

"Still alive back here?" he asked.

"Mm-hmm," Izzy mumbled without looking up from her tea.

He tried to reassure her. "I'm sure we can put everything back once the celebration's over."

"If it's not the outside, they'll find something else.

There's always something. It took the council nearly two years to approve my bees. Two years!" She clanged her teacup down on the metal table and looked up at him. "There's not another house for nearly a mile, but still, it was a battle just to get the first damned hive. Now, everyone in the town buys honey from us, but no one ever bothered to acknowledge the hoops they made us jump through. You should have seen the backlash when I bought the bakery building. I tore out a few walls, and the town nearly had a meltdown. The building was sitting empty, and they still couldn't stand for anyone to change it. I'm tired of fighting to be myself, kiddo. I'm getting too old for it. You know, I've thought of selling this place and maybe moving out west. Portland sounds pretty nice."

So the issue wasn't simply the outside of the building. Izzy was the nicest person he'd ever known, and he felt a flicker of anger at the thought of the unnecessary anguish placed upon her. He could see why Anna had seemed so irrationally upset.

"This place would be dull without you," he said. "It's still pretty dull with you in it. Clearly, they love your bakery, whether they'll admit it or not."

This didn't sound like him. *Blend in* was usually Oliver's motto, but the feeling he felt deep down in his belly was the same he'd felt before flipping over the clock in front of his entire office. He'd felt a twinge of it while standing in the back of the town-hall meeting. It wasn't just anger, though. Something else was there, too, a profound sense of sadness for just how much the need for others' approval dominated his life. *Stick out.* His subconscious pleaded with him. *Stick out like your happiness depends on it. Flip the freakin' clock.*

"Thanks, kiddo," Izzy said with a forced smile before returning to her tea.

Later that evening, Pan circled Nekko in the living room, yipping playfully and trying to get the fat cat to engage. Nekko stretched out on the rug and yawned, paying no attention to the mischievous corgi. She was an immovable force, a heavy boulder, until Pan started to nudge her with his cold nose. Nekko gave the pup a warning growl. He perked up his ears and backed away, not sure what to make of the strange noise coming from the orange lump on the floor. After a moment of hesitation, he decided to chance it and ran headfirst into the cat's soft, exposed underbelly. His actions resulted in a swift *thwap thwap* as Nekko rolled onto her hind legs and brought her massive front paws down onto Pan's head in quick succession. The dog yelped and ran into the other room. Fortunately, Nekko had been declawed, but the pup received the message loud and clear.

Oliver watched the action unfold from a papasan chair, where he sat with one of his aunt's sketchpads.

He'd never seen Nekko move that quickly before and was pretty sure he wouldn't see it again without the help of Pan's prodding. Izzy had gone to bed a while before, but Oliver couldn't shake the stench of the day, which left him wide awake and discontented. From the sounds of it, the council had been on Izzy's case for years and had made her life in Christchurch a constant battle. He wanted to do something to make her feel better. He felt complicit, not for something he had done but for something he hadn't. Instead of speaking up for his aunt, he'd stood idle, leaving Izzy and Anna flapping in the breeze. He wasn't sure what he could have said to help, but anything would have been better than nothing.

Oliver was a perpetual bystander. The same thing had happened a week before, when Jeanine needed a moment to grieve in peace and Mr. Sally scolded her for being away from the desk. It had happened in elementary school, when his classmates made fun of one of the new girls for her Coke-bottle glasses. His life was full of these moments, and he was determined not to slip back into his old habit of complacency. He sketched out an idea, a plan for something he would be able to pull off just in time for the tricentennial celebration.

CHAPTER SEVEN

"This is the most beautiful thing I've ever seen," Izzy said, holding the piece of sketch paper in one hand and cupping her mouth with the other. Her eyes glistened with tears. "I had no idea you sketched."

"Oh, please. I doodle a little, but I think you get the idea," Oliver replied.

His aunt leaned against the kitchen counter, scanning the sketch and taking in all the details. "Just tell me what you'll need to make it happen," she said.

"Just a few evenings of your time in order to finish it by the tricentennial," he replied. "I'll stop by the hardware store today and scope out all of the supplies."

Izzy placed the sketch on the table and wrapped her arms around him.

"Have I ever told you you're my favorite grand-nephew?" she asked.

"I thought I was the only one," he replied.

"That's beside the point. This made my day," she added. "I'll go see what I have in my studio. The revolution lives on!" she shouted, pumping her fist in the air and walking into the living room toward the staircase.

With the tricentennial only two days away, they had a lot of work to do and a very short amount of time in which to do it. Oliver cleared the old garage behind Izzy's house and pulled the blue station wagon inside. A line of spray-paint cans, all of different colors, sat on the makeshift workbench, next to several rolls of painter's tape. The next two days were a blur. After finishing their shifts at the bakery, Izzy and Oliver would return to the garage to work on the car. They carefully taped off portions of it to recreate the design from Oliver's sketch on the metal body. Painting the car was more work than initially anticipated, but the patterns slowly came together. While they worked in the garage, Pan busied himself chasing rolling spray cans across the floor. Nekko had the run of the entire house but barely moved from the windowsill in the kitchen.

Back at the bakery, Anna started work on the tricentennial cake. The mammoth confection consisted of three massive tiers. The bottom tier was made to look like a field of colorful wildflowers, mimicking those around the edges of the town. *Christchurch* was spelled out in rich chocolate lettering on the second tier, and a miniature recreation of the town sat atop the third. She paid special attention to the tiny bakery on the top tier and ensured the outer walls were covered with colorful designs, as they had been before Oliver took the hose to them.

After two days of baking and two nights of working in the garage, the morning of the tricentennial had arrived. Large wicker baskets of baked goods lined the metal table in the bakery kitchen, and several racks full of breads and pastries sat in waiting. They would load the baskets into Izzy's car, drive them to their booth in the square, then come back for more goodies as needed.

Izzy pulled the car around to the back door of the bakery and opened the trunk. "If this festival is anything like the annual festival last year, we'll be sold out by noon," she said.

Anna carried a basket of bread outside and stopped cold when she saw what had once been the robin-egg station wagon.

"And what is this?" she asked.

Bright swirls of color laced the sides of the car. A caricature in Izzy's likeness was prominently displayed on the hood, holding a rolling pin in the air as if daring the Elders to confront her. The Rolling Pin was spelled out in graffiti-style letters, spanning each side of the station wagon.

"If the town won't let us have a colorful store, we're going to have a colorful car," Izzy said. "It was Oliver's idea."

"I didn't know that you were an artist too," Anna told Oliver.

"Oh, I can draw a little, but I was mostly just the idea man," he replied.

"Nonsense," Izzy said. "You should have seen him paint. I think it's the most I've seen him smile since he's been here." She jabbed Oliver in the ribs with her elbow.

He did have an undernourished artistic flair, one that wasn't satiated by the engineering drawings he had been paid to crank out for Mr. Sally. He'd been happier in the last few days than he'd been for some time and noticed the bounce had returned to Izzy's step too. She'd come alive over the two nights in the garage, seemingly fueled by her rebellious spirit.

"And why didn't you tell me about this before-hand?" Anna asked. "You know how long I've been waiting to stick it to this town? I could have helped."

"We wanted it to be a surprise," Oliver said.

The town Elders had enlisted an army of volunteers to assemble the festival booths. The station wagon's wheels hummed on the uneven brick as Izzy cautiously drove past stacks of metal poles and canvas tent covers. The car garnered looks from the helpers as it passed in a rainbow blur. Izzy pulled up next to the bakery booth and ensured Oliver's design was front and center. In a sea of red-and-white canvas stripes, the wagon was an explosion of color, impossible for the eyes to miss.

Oliver and Anna lined several card tables with baskets of baked goods, while Izzy scrawled prices on a miniature chalkboard display and recreated her likeness from the hood of the car. Both she and her chalk caricatures were beaming. As visitors started to trickle in, several stopped to take pictures with the car, picking up a cinnamon roll or donut along the way. The station wagon not only served as a defiant act of self-expression, it turned out to be a great marketing tool as well.

"Interesting paint job. A little garish, don't you think?" Madeline strolled over to the bakery booth with a small entourage of Elder members following closely behind, like a flock of ducks forming a flying V. Oliver hadn't noticed it from a distance at the town-hall meeting, but Madeline wore a lapel pin bearing the seal of the Elders, as did the gaggle standing behind her.

"No rules against painting your car, are there Madeline? Or are you planning to address that at the next meeting?" Izzy turned her back on the woman and pretended to rearrange the bakery baskets.

"You know, there's a reason why we have these

rules. People come to this town expecting a certain look, an historic look. They don't come to be visually assaulted with junkyard sculptures and spray paint," she said, eyes darting to the station wagon.

Anna also had her back turned to the group. She said nothing but accidentally took her anger out on a baguette, which she snapped in half on the edge of the table.

Oliver felt as if he were standing back in the old office, with his boss's finger wagging in his face. He was done being wagged at. He had been wagged at his entire life. He forced a smile and locked eyes with Madeline. "So, what can I get for you today? A cookie? A piece of bread to feed your flock?" He gestured toward the other women.

Madeline's eyes narrowed, but she struggled to find an adequate comeback. She turned without saying another word, and the group strolled away in synchronized step.

As the Elders made their way down the aisle of booths, he looked over at the basket of rolls next to him. Before he could stop himself, he picked up a roll, cocked his arm, and threw. Izzy turned just in time to see the roll leave Oliver's hand and fly toward the group of Elders. He had aimed for the back of Madeline's head, but his athletic track record was poor, and the roll veered to the left and grazed the shoulder of one of the other Elders. The woman swatted at her shoulder, as if to shoo a bug away, and turned around to see what had hit her. After a few confused moments, she returned to her place in the formation.

Izzy put a hand on Oliver's shoulder. He was clenching the table, and the knuckles on both of his hands were completely white. He looked over at her, pulled from his momentary rage.

"Sorry," he said. "I don't know what got into me. I shouldn't have done that." Embarrassment filled his cheeks with crimson. He could have caused a lot of heartache for Izzy, had the roll hit its intended target.

"Use a muffin next time. There's less wind deflection, and they hurt a hell of a lot more," she said, patting him on the shoulder.

The crowd grew larger throughout the morning, slowly shuffling in from the corners of the square. Oliver watched as lines of tourists followed little old ladies down the cobblestone side streets, taking in stories of the tiny village's past. Christchurch must have been a regular stop for history buffs. Little had changed in the town square since the initial buildings went up, indoor plumbing aside. The town had also won Village of the Year awards, which the council displayed prominently in the town hall's trophy cases.

Several thousand people descended on Christchurch for the day, which brought booming business. Izzy, Oliver, and Anna rotated between the booth and the store and were completely sold out by early afternoon, just as Izzy had predicted.

The tricentennial cake was to be unveiled at the mayor's lunchtime address, and volunteers had cordoned off the area surrounding the founder's statue and placed a podium at his feet. Anna had wheeled the cake over to the council booth earlier in the day, and the council members kept it hidden from view behind a red velvet curtain.

"If I could have everyone's attention," the mayor said, tapping on the microphone.

The chatter died down to a low hum.

"First of all, I would like to welcome you to Christchurch and thank all of you for coming. And a very special thanks to the volunteers who made this festival possible!" The crowd cheered. "I'd also like to thank the town council and our dedicated group of Elders." The mayor paused for additional applause.

After the long list of thank-yous, he pulled back the velvet curtain and unveiled the cake to a wide range of "oohs" and "ahhhs." Izzy, Oliver, and Anna stood next to him, and Anna was beaming from the crowd's response. The mayor walked down the line, shaking Izzy's hand, shaking Oliver's hand, then embracing Anna in a warm hug.

"Nicely done, sweetie," he said.

Oliver hadn't been impressed by the town Elders, but the mayor had an aura of compassion and authenticity about him. Although he was an enforcer of the town rules, Oliver had a feeling the man didn't necessarily agree with all the Elders' actions.

After the unveiling, Oliver and Izzy returned to the bakery, which had become a place of respite for the festival volunteers and weary travelers. Izzy whipped up a few fresh batches of baked goods, while Oliver kept the coffee brewing and flowing into the cups of the town patrons.

"More coffee?" he asked a man sitting in one of the booths and reading a newspaper.

"Sure! You're Oliver, right? Don't believe we've met yet. My name's Martin." The man was short in stature and wore a light-brown suit and maroon sweater. His head was absent of any hair and looked as if it had been shined by an industrial floor buffer.

"That's right. Nice to meet you. What do you do around here?"

"I run the antique shop on the other side of the square. You may have met my wife, Madeline," he replied.

Oliver struggled to maintain his smile and cheery demeanor.

"I've had the pleasure," he said.

Martin seemed to pick up on Oliver's underlying

emotions and chuckled. "She takes her role pretty seriously. I know she gives your aunt a hard time, but she's got good intentions. You know, you should come by the pub after cleanup. We usually meet there for a few pints before calling it a night. Might be a good opportunity to meet some of the townsfolk in a more casual setting," he said, giving Oliver a wink.

A wave from a booth at the other side of the room caught Oliver's attention.

"I'll be there," he said. "I've gotta run, but it was nice to meet you. I'll have to stop by the shop one day."

"Please do. It was great to meet you too," Martin said, returning to his paper.

Oliver made another round with the coffee pot before returning to the kitchen to rest for a bit. The kitchen looked as if a flour bomb had gone off inside, and the veritable war zone was filled with dirty pans and splatters of dough. His cup of coffee had gotten cold, but he took a swig anyway, hoping the caffeine would provide the boost of energy needed to power through the rest of the day.

"Just met Madeline's husband," he said.

Izzy stuck her head out from behind a bakery rack.

"Like oil and vinegar those two, don't you think?" she asked.

"He was so friendly. I just don't get how someone like that could be married to *her*."

"To each their own, I guess," she said, lifting a tray of baked goods from the rack and emptying it into a basket.

"He mentioned a meet up at the pub after festival cleanup. Are you going?"

"Oh, I never go to those things. Not my crowd, really," Izzy replied.

"And what is your crowd, exactly?" he asked.

"I'll let you know if I ever figure that out."

CHAPTER EIGHT

The Horseman sat in the corner of the square, diagonal from the bakery and across the dirt road from the market. The building had been constructed in the late seventeen hundreds, according to the plaque next to the entrance, and had scars from the Revolutionary War, including a cannonball wedged in one of its walls. The white wooden shingles appeared to have just received a fresh coat of paint, and the picket fence cordoned off a carefully manicured courtyard patio and garden.

At first, Izzy refused to cross the square to the tavern and only relented after Anna committed to going as well.

"It's crazy how quickly the town cleared out," Oliver said. The bakery cleanup had taken several hours, but he was still surprised the square had been cleared in such a short amount of time.

"That's because there's nowhere to spend the night," Anna replied. "The tavern is the town's only inn, and it's only got a few rooms. The council's had a few proposals from hotel franchises, but they felt a hotel would be out of place and inauthentic. So visitors either go home or stay in the neighboring town. Such a wasted opportunity. Everyone from Christchurch, on the other hand, celebrates at the tavern."

The Horseman's ceiling was low. The lights were dim, and dark wood paneling accented the cozy interior. A roaring fire fought off the crisp evening air.

The trio sat at a booth off to the right of the bar. The place had a social buzz about it—an energy that carried over from the festival. Oliver squeezed his way to the bar to order a beer for himself and Anna and a glass of honey wine for Izzy.

"Good to see you again," said someone from the stool next to him.

Oliver had been so busy trying to grab the bartender's attention that he hadn't noticed Martin sitting next to him on a barstool. "Good to see you too," he replied.

"Oliver, this is my friend Harry," he said, gesturing to the man on the stool next to him. "He runs the local music shop. Keeps all our little ones supplied with instruments."

"Good to meet you," Harry said, giving Oliver a nod.

"What can I get for ya?" the bartender asked loudly in Oliver's ear, catching him by surprise.

Oliver turned and ordered.

"How long will you be in town for?" Harry asked.

"Not sure yet," Oliver replied. "Still have some things to figure out back home."

"Well, all of the guys get together to play cards here on Wednesdays. You ought to come join us sometime."

"I'd love to."

That was the second time that day Oliver had been caught off guard by genuine hospitality, and he'd resolved to say yes to any opportunities to get to know the townspeople. His first experience at the town hall had been so jarring that he'd been quick to judge them, but perhaps Madeline wasn't representative of the people in Christchurch after all.

"It was nice to meet you, Harry," he said. He paid his tab and returned to the booth.

Izzy had ranted about the town being full of cookie-cutter automatons, but Oliver noticed that even she was making small talk with a group of men as they passed her booth.

Oliver set the drinks on the table and slid into the booth next to Izzy.

"Just met Harry. Seems like a pretty friendly guy. Invited me to play cards," Oliver said.

"His wife is one of the Elders, you know. Could be using you to try to get to me," Izzy said, taking a sip of the deep-amber wine. "Just be careful."

"I don't know if conspiratorial relationship building is a part of the Elder agenda. Seems a bit far-fetched," he replied.

"Oh, you laugh now, but you won't be laughing when they pass some kind of special tax on muffins that drives us out of business. You're going to have to let me and Pan come live with you in the city," she said. "And be forewarned—Pan snores."

Living on the edge of social acceptance had apparently led Izzy to develop a few wild beliefs. She also believed the moon landing had been faked and the town was secretly poisoning her bees.

"Just look at them," she added, nodding her head toward the back corner of the tavern.

Madeline sat in the center seat of a circular booth, surrounded by other Elders. Everyone had ordered glasses of red wine, which sat in oddly perfect symmetry on the wooden table. The light from the fire flashed off the group's matching pewter lapel pins.

"Automatons."

Izzy's paranoid aura died down by the third glass of wine, and she and Anna got lost in a discussion about updates to the bakery menu.

After several minutes of listening to their conversation, Oliver caught himself dozing off. He looked at the three empty pint glasses on the table in front of him and realized someone would have to carry him home if he stayed much longer.

"And where do you think you're going?" Izzy asked as Oliver stood to leave.

"Going to stop by the bakery and grab some stuff for breakfast," he said. Amid all the work leading up to the festival, he'd neglected to stop by the market, and the cupboards were bare at home.

"Be careful. We'll be home in a bit," Izzy said.

The square was dark and had already been picked clean of litter. Striped booth canvases and tent poles lay neatly stacked at the square's perimeter, where they would be hauled away in the morning.

Oliver crossed the square, wobbling from a combination of beer and exhaustion. He saluted the founder statue as he passed and chuckled.

He decided to take the alleyway to the back of the bakery. A single floodlight lit the narrow path. As Oliver entered the alley, he noticed a crumpled form on the ground ahead of him, illuminated by the overhead light. At first, he thought the shape was a bag of trash, but upon closer inspection, the object came into focus. A person was lying limp in the damp walkway.

The warm glow of the alcohol was gone in an instant, with the hunched body delivering an effective dose of sobriety. "It" was a "she," and the woman was oddly positioned, sitting up, with both legs out and head slumped over in her lap.

"Are you all right?" he asked, kneeling down next to her. He placed a hand on her shoulder. When she didn't respond, panic set in. He brushed his index finger against her cheek. *Still warm.* "I'm going to lay you back, okay?" He had no idea if she could hear him. A gentle tug on her shoulders caused the woman to fall backward, upsetting the delicate balance that had allowed her to sit in such an awkward position.

Her eyes were wide open and unflinching. Oliver had seen people with cataracts before, but her eyes were completely gray, like glass that had been fogged over. Her mouth hung slack-jawed at an odd angle. *Her jaw's been dislocated.* The realization made him nauseous. She stared at the dark sky above, no sign of life left in her body. He turned toward the pub and ran, nearly tripping over his own feet.

The door to the tavern burst open with such force that it caused the entire room to stop midsentence and turn toward Oliver.

"There's a body. I think she's dead! Help!" he said,

panting from the mix of fright, overexertion, and alcohol. Gasps came from the onlookers, and several jumped up from their seats to follow him back to the scene. Most sat, frozen in shock, but Izzy and Anna hopped to their feet and ran to him.

He led the group of pubgoers across the square and into the alley.

"She's over here." He gestured as he sprinted to where the woman's body lay splayed on the ground.

As he looked down at the body, he noticed something he hadn't before—a lapel pin. Although her face had been deformed, he realized the woman on the ground had been the unfortunate victim of his bread attack earlier that day. He stumbled backward against the wall and retched.

Joy gave way to terror as the rest of the revelers from the tavern poured out onto the street. Oliver sat back against the wall, staring at the scene in front of him. Anna knelt down next to him, not daring to look at the body.

Martin had been one of the first to arrive and approached the woman. "Oh, Jesus," he muttered under his breath as Harry approached from behind. Martin turned and blocked Harry's view.

"Harry," he said, gripping the man's shoulder to keep him from going any farther. His voice trembled.

"What is it?" Harry asked.

"It's... it's Francis." He stared down at Harry's Oxfords as he delivered the news.

"What, is she okay?"

Harry tried to push him aside, but Martin side-stepped in front of him. Harry had a good foot in height on Martin, but Martin seemed determined to keep Harry from seeing his wife's disfigured face. The image was burned into Oliver's mind, and he was happy that Martin was attempting to spare Harry the mental anguish.

A crowd had gathered at the mouth of the alleyway, watching the scuffle between the two men.

"Move out of my way," Harry said, this time forcefully pushing Martin aside.

"Call Eric," Martin said to Izzy, who rushed off to the back of the bakery.

He caught up with Harry, who had already taken several steps forward. At first, he seemed unsure of what he was looking at, but the shape of Francis's body must have slowly come into focus, the Elder pin sparkling in the lamplight. Harry fell to his knees.

Martin put his hand on Harry's shoulder. "Come on. Come back here. You don't need to see this." He started to pull the man back toward him, but Harry jerked free.

"Get away from me!" he shouted, leaning over to embrace his wife. He lifted her limp body from the ground and held her face against his chest. Harry let out a deep moan, but it sounded as if it came from both man and wife, the grand death rattle of a forty-year relationship.

Several minutes later, a man pushed his way toward the alley, parting the crowd. He wore a tan overcoat with a woolen sweater and appeared to have just been pulled from a deep slumber. He approached Harry and placed a hand on his shoulder. "Let's see what happened. We'll take good care of her, I promise."

Harry hugged his wife tightly before gingerly setting her corpse down on the ground as if to prevent further injury. The man in the overcoat must have caught a glimpse of the woman's face, because he let out an audible gasp that he attempted to stifle by clearing his throat. He muttered something to Harry and knelt with him until two additional officers arrived at the scene.

The man snapped his fingers to get the attention of one of the officers. "Looks like she was running toward the pub. Take a statement from Harry, and get Will to head over to the house and take a look before you let him go home."

"Come with me, Harry. We just need a quick word," the officer said, trying to guide him away from the body. "It'll be okay. You'll see her again. I'll be quick."

As the officer guided a shell-shocked Harry away from the body, the man in the overcoat turned his attention toward Oliver.

"You must be the one who found her. Oliver, isn't it?" he asked.

Oliver nodded in silent affirmation.

The man held out his hand. "I'm Eric," he said, "the chief of police of Christchurch. Tell me what happened."

"I just found her like this, slumped over on the ground," Oliver replied.

"What about you? Did you two see anything?" he asked Anna.

She shook her head. "Izzy and I came with the rest of the crowd after he ran to the pub for help."

Oliver recounted the story several times as Eric tried to glean any useful information about what might have happened to the poor woman. But Oliver had witnessed nothing more than the same crumpled body on display for everyone to see.

Izzy returned from the bakery, carrying a large glass of water. "Did they find anything?" she asked, handing the glass to Oliver.

"They're talking to Harry now. No one has seen anything," Anna replied.

One of the officers—Will, Oliver presumed—came

running from the other end of the alley. "You have to come and see this!" he shouted.

Eric turned to the other officer, who was preoccupied with Harry, then turned back to Oliver. "You're going to have to come with me since we're a bit limited on manpower. I have a few more questions for you."

"Can we do anything to help?" Izzy asked.

"We've got things under control here. We'll be in touch tomorrow. You two go home and get some rest," he replied.

He helped Oliver regain his footing then followed Will down the alley to Francis's house.

The two-story cottage looked as if it had been picked out of a travel magazine and plopped on the street. The lawn was perfectly manicured, and flower boxes hung from each of the windows. Although the house was perfect at first glance, Oliver noticed a deep crack down the center of the bright-red front door.

Eric stopped and furrowed his brow. "Do you know how much force it would take to do this?" he asked. "It's solid wood."

"Take a look inside," Will replied.

"Stay here," Eric said to Oliver. He carefully pushed the door open. A scene of complete destruction greeted them on the other side. The entire living room and kitchen had been torn apart. The wooden table lay in a broken heap on the floor, and shards of glass and debris speckled the carpet in the living room. Oliver couldn't see all the chaos through the doorframe, but he did notice that some of the cupboard doors in the kitchen had been nearly ripped from their hinges and hung loosely like baby teeth.

The scene looked as if someone had taken a sledge-hammer to the place. A chill ran up Oliver's spine as he realized whoever had caused the damage must still be running around Christchurch.

Oliver walked back to the sidewalk. The lights in most of the neighboring houses were off. With most people at the tavern, no one would have been home to hear her cries for help if she had been running from someone.

After a few minutes inside, Eric appeared in the doorway, with Will close behind. "We're going to need more people than I thought. Get in touch with the station in the next town over."

CHAPTER NINE

"A heart attack?" Oliver couldn't believe it.

The writeup in the local paper was laughable. After a brief investigation, it was determined Francis had a major heart attack and must have hit her head during the fall in the alley. *But what did she hit her head on?* Oliver had found Francis's body in the middle of the alley, nowhere near any objects that could have caused her jaw to nearly come loose from her face during a fall.

"There's just no way a fall could have done that," he said. "And the look on her face—it looked as if she had been scared to death."

"She was old, and old people fall. Freak accidents happen," Izzy said. "I nearly fall down the steps every day, and my skin bruises if you look at it the wrong way." She walked over to a green cupboard sitting in the corner of the kitchen and returned with a bottle.

"Here," she said. "Have a little Irish with your coffee. It'll take your mind off all of this."

She poured a healthy splash into Oliver's mug, and the cream swirled into his coffee, turning it from black to a milky beige. It was a bit more *Irish* than he had anticipated.

He looked up from the coffee cup. "What about the house, then? The place was in complete shambles—like a tornado had ripped through it."

The paper had an answer for that too. The police had found no evidence of breaking and entering and no fingerprints or signs of foul play. Although this didn't explain how Francis could have caused such a mess, it did seem to explain away the possibility that someone else had.

"What are you suggesting then, that she was murdered?" Izzy asked. "There hasn't been a murder in this town for as long as I can remember."

"I don't know. Maybe someone followed her home from the festival. Maybe she interrupted a burglary. There's no way that this could have been an accident," he said.

"The police didn't find anything. Maybe Francis caused the mess during the panic of her heart attack. If she had been murdered, don't you think they would have found some scrap of evidence? Anyway, those sorts of things just don't happen here. You've got to let it go." She put one hand on Oliver's. "I know what you saw was traumatic, and the brain tends to make fairy tales out of trauma. No one wants to think it's possible for someone to just keel over, but it happens. It's unfair, but there's nothing more to it than that—no evil forces and certainly no murder."

"I guess you're right," Oliver said, having a flashback of Maurice flipping over in his office.

A FEW WEEKS PASSED, and the town slowly returned to normal, with the exception of Madeline. Ever since Oliver discovered Francis's body in the alley, she had been on a warpath. Although he couldn't settle for the official story either, he was fairly certain Madeline held him personally responsible for Francis's death. In the weeks following the incident in the alley, the bakery had been subjected to a surprise health inspection and another unusual lull in business. This hadn't been discussed in a town-hall meeting, so Izzy had no one to appeal to. It was an underground effort that stayed strictly off the books. Oliver imagined a series of late-night phone calls and discreet tavern conversations, things that left no paper trail. He couldn't prove Madeline had been responsible, but the timing was just too coincidental. Izzy's conspiratorial thinking was starting to rub off on him.

The drama had taken a toll on Anna's relationship with her father as well. She hadn't been herself for several days, and her declining mood was starting to impact those around her. Oliver and Izzy tried to cheer her up to no avail. After a bit of prodding, Oliver got Anna to admit her sourness was the result of a huge argument she and her father had gotten into over the town's treatment of Oliver and the bakery even though she remained tightlipped about the specifics.

"What did that bread ever do to you?" Oliver asked as Anna stood at the table underneath the tree mosaic and pounded a ball of dough with her rolling pin. She looked down at the rubbery mess, sighed, and slid the lump into the trash bin.

"Must have zoned out," she said, dismissing the question.

"Can I help with anything?" he asked.

Anna turned around and pointed the rolling pin at Oliver. "You can stay out of my way and let me do my job," she snapped.

Sitting on the stool at the large metal table, Izzy looked up from her accounting sheets, raising her eyebrows at Oliver. She'd clearly chosen not to push

Anna's buttons and resolved to let the girl work her issues out through the dough.

"All right, all right," he replied, recoiling from the angry response. "I think it would be good if you got some fresh air. You're scaring me a little."

"I've got too much to do," Anna replied.

"He's right. Go get some fresh air, and take Oliver with you. I think I can hold down the fort here." Izzy gestured toward the empty storefront. "And drop this basket off at Harry's. The poor man could probably use a fresh bite to eat."

"I can't. I have to redo this loaf."

"It wasn't a request," Izzy replied.

She rarely gave direct commands, so Anna set the rolling pin on the table and folded up her apron. Anna and Oliver left through the back door and walked along the street behind the bakery.

"I'm sorry," she said after a few strained moments of silence. "I'm just so angry. This isn't fair. We did nothing wrong. You had nothing to do with Francis's death. Even the police said so. Why do they always have to come for us, for Izzy?"

"I'm sure Madeline doesn't actually believe I had anything to do with it," Oliver said. "She's just grieving and clearly has no other way to deal with it aside from being a huge bitch." He didn't typically swear, so that line made Anna giggle. "This will pass, and everything will go back to normal eventually."

"Until the next infraction," she added. "It's been a never-ending cycle since I started working here."

"I think Izzy likes being a one-woman rebellion. What fun would it be for her without the drama?" he asked.

They arrived at Francis's several minutes later. The door had been braced in the center with a piece of lumber clumsily screwed in and bridging the large crack. Several weeks had passed, but Harry hadn't bothered to have it replaced. He hadn't bothered to do much of anything, and Oliver hadn't seen him in public in days. He didn't blame Harry—he would have locked himself away to grieve in peace as well.

They walked the stone path to the front door.

"He probably doesn't want to be bothered," he said. "Maybe we can just leave it on his doorstep."

"We'll just ring the bell and leave it if he doesn't answer," she replied.

She pressed the doorbell. Oliver looked up at the heavy splintered door and examined the large split in the wood. The feat seemed impossible for an old woman... or anyone, for that matter.

They waited for a minute or so, but no one came. They would have to leave the basket and hope for the best. As he knelt to set the basket on the steps, he noticed a small metal object protruding from the mulch bed next to the door. The view had been obstructed by the hedgerow, but Oliver could see the object clearly from that angle. He reached underneath the bush and plucked it from the dirt.

"Look at this," he said, holding it out for Anna to see.

"What is it?"

"It's some kind of metal coin, but I can't make out what's on it," he replied.

The edges were smooth but irregular, and it had the appearance of tarnished gold. Oliver handed it to Anna, who attempted to wipe away the dirt filling the crevices of the coin. She held it close to her eye to get a closer look at the spiraling designs on its face.

"They look like vines," she said. "And that's a bird tangled in them."

The door creaked, startling Anna, and she dropped the coin on the ground.

Harry stood in the doorway, wearing a pair of cotton pajamas and a five-o'clock shadow that appeared to be more ten o'clock in nature.

"Anna, Oliver... what can I do for you?" he asked, forcing a smile.

"Sorry to bother you. We just thought you might like some bread and a few cinnamon rolls." Anna picked up the basket and handed it to him.

"That's very kind of you," he said. He looked down at the basket. "Thought of stopping by the bakery this week but just couldn't bring myself to do it." The man's eyes went glossy.

"It's okay. Whenever you want to drop in, we're happy to have you. If you need anything, you just say the word," Anna said.

"I appreciate it. I've got to be going, but thanks for stopping by." Harry started to push the door shut.

"Take care," she said.

"Harry, wait," Oliver said. "Before you go, we found this under the hedges. Is it yours?" He bent down to pick up the coin and handed it to Harry.

Harry flipped the coin around in his hand.

"Nope, can't say that I've seen it before. Looks like money of some kind. Maybe Martin can tell you what it is. Take care now," he said, handing the coin back to Oliver and gingerly shutting the broken door.

"Poor man," Anna said.

"I can't imagine what he's going through," Oliver replied. "Well, back to the bakery?"

"What do you say we stop at the antique shop on the way? Harry has a good point. If anyone in this town knows anything about the coin, it's probably Martin. I'm sure he would be willing to take a look for us. Could be a fun little distraction. The bakery isn't exactly booming today."

CHAPTER TEN

Fletcher Antiquities sat directly across the square from the bakery. The storefront was made of delicately carved woodwork painted a deep maroon, and the large bay window gave a preview of all the treasures hidden within. Once inside, they walked toward the back of the store, passing a hodgepodge of metal lanterns suspended from the ceiling. Paintings and family portraits hung from the walls, obscured by antique furniture that jutted out into the aisle. Knick-knacks of various shapes and sizes sat in containers atop the furniture, and precious necklaces lay draped across old cigar boxes and ashtrays. The place was filled to the brim as if the owner were a raccoon and the store was his den of shiny stolen bobbles.

Martin sat watch at an old mahogany desk in the back of the store. He was scribbling something in a

ledger with a fancy-looking fountain pen when Oliver
and Anna approached.

"Good to see you two. What brings you in?" he
asked, looking up from his work.

"We were hoping you could take a look at this coin
for us," Anna said, as Oliver was distracted by a large
glass case of especially valuable trinkets.

At one end of the case, a beautiful ruby ring sat in
the middle of a delicate gold necklace, and at the other,
several fountain pens were fanned out on a pad of soft
purple velvet.

"Sure! Let's have a look, then," Martin replied.

Oliver was still lost in the antiques, and Anna
jabbed him with her elbow.

"Oh, uh, sorry," he said, handing Martin the coin.

Martin opened one of the desk drawers and pulled
out a small eyepiece, which he wedged between his
brow and cheekbone and held in place with a squint.
He flipped the coin over in his hand and examined the
etching on its surface.

"Huh," he said. "Never seen a coin like this before.
Where did you find it?"

"Sticking out of a flower bed," Oliver replied.

Martin sat back in his chair. "You know, I have
seen *something* like this before, but not in coin form."
He pulled a small ring of keys from his pocket, rose
from his chair, and turned toward the narrow door

next to him, which looked as if it led to a broom closet.

"This is my own little private collection." He beamed, sliding one of the keys into the lock. "The town once had a small printing press, believe it or not. The press is long gone now, but I've managed to find copies of nearly every book that it ever printed—a bit of a passion project of mine, actually."

The small room was just wide enough to fit a set of narrow bookshelves against one wall while leaving a small path on the other. Martin traced his finger along a row of leather spines until he found the book he'd been searching for. The book was clad in deep-brown leather and embossed with golden lettering.

"This is one of my favorites." He pulled the book from the shelf and brought it back to his work desk. Then he gestured for Oliver and Anna to take a seat. "Shortly before the town's founder, Samuel Hale, passed, the townsfolk made a concerted effort to capture the town's history. He'd been the story keeper, and they didn't want tales of Christchurch's early days to be lost when he died."

Martin carefully opened the front cover and flipped through the pages.

"Samuel was actually a twin, believe it or not. He and his brother founded the town in 1719–something most people around here aren't quick to acknowledge and seem eager to forget, but things quickly went sour. Samuel was a pious man, obsessed with order, obedience, and the cross. His brother, Nathaniel, on the other hand, had a wild streak about him. Samuel even accused his brother of being a male witch and claimed he had tried to sabotage his efforts to keep order in the town. Apparently, the doors in the town jail cells would come open sporadically. Livestock would vanish, and Samuel even returned home one day to discover all of his family's belongings neatly stacked on the roof of his home. No one was ever caught red-handed, so the next logical explanation, at least at the time, was witchcraft. Of course, accusations of witchcraft were still *en vogue*, and the penalties of being found a witch were well documented, so instead of staying and risking his life, Nathaniel fled. That's when things get a bit fuzzy. Samuel claimed he caught up with Nathaniel, who'd become snagged in a briar patch at the edge of the woods. According to him, the patch slowly wrapped itself around his brother as if it were some sort of carnivorous beast. Samuel thought it was God's way of punishing Nathaniel for his misdeeds—as any good brother would do—so he stood there and watched. A great Christian indeed, eh?"

Martin pointed at a picture in the book. The image showed a struggling Nathaniel reaching a hand out toward his brother, who sat on horseback next to the pit of briars.

"But it didn't end there for Nathaniel, and what happens next somewhat suggests he may have actually been a witch or, more likely, his brother was a liar. Samuel said the tree line had been speckled with crows and his brother reached toward them, as if pulling them from the trees with an invisible grip. A swirling murder formed overhead and descended upon the briars like some sort of feathered tornado, plunging into the thorns and sacrificing themselves to save Nathaniel."

Martin flipped the page. A crow lay entangled in a patch of bloody briars, wings crushed by the tensing branches. He set the coin on top of the picture. "Seem familiar?"

"So, what happened to Nathaniel?" Oliver asked.

"He disappeared, never to be seen again. Possible, I guess. I think it's more likely Samuel and a few of the townsfolk may have subjected him to an unofficial trial. One doesn't typically survive tests for witchcraft, and survival only indicated guilt. No, I think his brother murdered him. It didn't go over well with some of the townsfolk either, and several started to disappear after Nathaniel's departure, starting with Nathaniel's wife and child. According to Samuel, several deserted after his brother fled, likely guilty of witchcraft themselves.

It's also possible they started to ask too many questions, and he found it easier to do away with them—that or they realized his delusion and left of their own accord. A few accounts do exist of missing livestock, rations, and tools from around that time, so it's possible they did escape to the woods. Whether it was exile or secret execution, Samuel wasn't exactly the benevolent force the town makes him out to be. Don't tell anyone I said that, though. Madeline would have my head."

Martin flipped the cover of the book closed and handed the coin back to Oliver. "I have no idea where this came from, though. The town did have its own currency, of which I have a complete collection, but this isn't like any of those coins. I doubt people would have been eager to commemorate an exiled witch, but the coin is old and certainly made of gold. Perhaps one of the owners of the town mint had a little vanity project on the side." Martin leaned forward. "Would love to add this to my collection. If you ever decide you'd be interested in selling it, promise me you'll bring it back here first. I think I could make a fair offer."

"After all the help that you've given us, you can count on it," Oliver said. "But if it's worth something, we'd just give it back to Harry. We found it in his yard, after all."

Martin's smile faded. "Have you spoken to the poor fellow recently?"

"Just dropped off a basket of baked goods this morning," Anna replied.

"How's he holding up?"

"Doesn't seem to be doing too well. We were surprised he answered the door," she said.

"I stopped by the other day, but he didn't answer. Figured he just wanted to be left alone for a while. Can't imagine what he's going through." He paused. "Well, do keep me in the loop with the coin. It's a pretty nifty find. Thanks for bringing it in, and feel free to have a look around before you go."

"One more thing, Martin. Any idea where that briar patch was located?" Oliver asked. "The one from the story, that is."

"Not exactly, but there's a huge patch near the edge of the woods on the outskirts of town. Should be right past your aunt's house, actually. The tree line's been in the same place for centuries," he said. "There's no other place like it near town, so my guess is that it's the same one from the story."

Once outside the store, Oliver could hardly contain his excitement. "Have you heard that story about the town before?" he asked.

"No, never," Anna replied. "I mean, I knew a little bit about Samuel's life, but no one ever mentioned his brother may have been exiled or murdered. I can see why. It doesn't necessarily paint Samuel in a positive light."

"This town does have a habit of believing what it wants despite the evidence," he replied.

Although the official line was that Francis had died of a heart attack, the court of public opinion clearly believed otherwise. Even though Oliver was firm in his own innocence, the suspicious in power had nearly shuttered Izzy's shop as a passive-aggressive form of retribution.

CHAPTER ELEVEN

P an lay underneath Izzy's feet as she sat on the porch. His legs were splayed out to the sides as if he were impersonating a bearskin rug. Izzy slid her glasses farther down her nose and held the coin out at arm's length until it came into focus.

"Martin says it's a reference to the town founder's twin," Oliver said.

"Nathaniel Hale," Izzy said, handing the coin back to Oliver

"That's right. So you know the story?"

"Ha! Know it? The story provided me a great deal of inspiration. Come with me, and I'll show you," she said, standing up and waiting for Oliver.

He tucked the coin into his pocket and followed her to the studio upstairs, with Pan close on their heels.

Oliver had never been inside Izzy's studio before, but he'd seen plenty of her paintings strewn about the house. Her work was full of color and whimsy, mostly exaggerated caricatures and obscure landscapes. She had even painted a larger-than-life portrait of Pan, using solely the pup's own paw prints.

Izzy stood on a chair outside her studio, reached up to the sill of the transom window, and pulled a skeleton key from atop the frame.

"Worried someone's going to steal your masterpieces?" he asked.

"Oh, you joke, but it's a legitimate concern. I do most of my painting here, but it's also where I keep my most-controversial works," she replied, straight-faced.

Sometimes, he found her self-importance comical. She pushed the door open to reveal a room lined with half-finished canvases and piles of paint tubes.

A mammoth canvas on the opposite wall immediately caught Oliver's attention. The abstract shapes, deep lines, and dark color palette took several moments to decode, but an interpretation of the scene from Martin's book slowly emerged. An obscure representation of who must have been Nathaniel Hale lay entangled in a briar patch, reaching up to the heavens for help. Samuel sat at a safe distance on horseback, watching his brother's agony with little emotion. Cubist crows circled overhead, blotting out the sun.

"You mean, you don't think the Elders would want to hang this up in the town hall?" Oliver joked. "I can see why you might keep this out of sight. It reminds me of Picasso's *Guernica*. It's incredible!"

"I consider it to be one of my most influential pieces," she said, rubbing her chin between her thumb and index finger, in clear appreciation of her own genius. "I brought it to the town art show, and it didn't go over very well. Turns out the town's all about the sanitized bits of its history, but things like this are only found hidden on bookshelves in Martin's shop. Needless to say, I think this may have put me on the wrong side of the Elders for good. Nothing's been the same since that art show. I liked to think my work was illuminating, but I don't think Madeline appreciated being illuminated."

Several works hung around the room, all of which portrayed a less-than-desirable image of the pious founder. One painting depicted the statue in the town square covered in bird poop. Another seemed to be a caricature of Madeline leaning over a large wooden desk and shouting at the observer. She'd been given a donkey-like mouth with an unflattering overbite.

Oliver had an idea as to why the Elders had problems with Izzy, but the paintings shed new light on Madeline's venomous attitude toward her. Izzy had actively declared war on the town's history and even Madeline herself.

"So, to answer your question, I know quite a bit about the story, whether the town likes it or not. And on that note, I'm off to bed. We've got a big order to fill for the school tomorrow, so I suggest you do the same."

"Wait, what about the coin? Do you have any idea where it may have come from?" he asked.

"Oh, sorry. No clue, but it's not often that I get to show off my work to people who might appreciate it," she replied. She patted him on the shoulder and began to leave the room.

"I think I'm going to stay up for a while," he said. "Not really tired at the moment."

"Be sure to lock the studio once you're done."

He returned to the large canvas, which depicted Nathaniel Hale's run-in with the briars. The events of the day bounced around his brain and refused to allow his mind to rest. *Where did the coin come from?*

Oliver squinted at the briar patch in the painting. If all the events from the story had actually taken place, Martin said there was a good chance it all went down right over the hill and across the field. He hadn't noticed it upon first inspection, but the forest in the painting seemed to be beckoning Nathaniel, branches reaching out toward him and the patch that held him in place. A hollow cavern had formed in the center of the trees, a dark passage into the unknown beyond. He admired it for several moments before locking up the studio and going to the kitchen to grab a flashlight.

The crisp night air hit his face as he stepped out onto the porch. The temperature had dropped several degrees since sunset, and the brisk evening breeze sent an invigorating chill through his body. The bright moon hung in the clear sky, illuminating the field below and casting subtle lunar rays through the mist hovering just above the ground. The tree line sat a mile or so away from the house, down the hill and through the field. He walked past the bee hives, which sat in perfectly placed rows. The inhabitants were fast asleep, or at least he assumed bees slept. Either way, the bees weren't a threat. The field below had been covered in brilliant patches of violet, yellow, and green during the day, but the colors had all faded to a dull gray under the moonlight. He reached the edge of the forest in fifteen minutes and was somewhat disappointed to find it wasn't nearly as ominous as it had appeared in Izzy's painting. He walked along the wilderness and traced its border with his flashlight. He wasn't prepared to stray too far into the woods but hoped to get at least a glimpse of the briar patch, if it existed. In reality, he expected to find nothing. *What are the odds that the same patch has survived for several hundred years?*

Martin had said the patch lay on the outskirts of town, and Oliver figured it shouldn't be difficult to spot. Within twenty minutes of leaving the house, Oliver stumbled upon the thorny pit he'd been looking for. The patch sat a few feet behind the tree line and blocked access to the deeper forest beyond. As he swept his flashlight back and forth, he noticed several red blooms, which appeared to be wild roses. Although he knew very little of plants, his grandfather had had a wild rosebush in his yard growing up, and Oliver would sometimes help him trim it as boy. Every now and then, he would scratch his hand on a thorn and burst into tears, but his grandpa seemed immune to the pain. After living through two wars, the man wasn't afraid of a little pinprick.

The roses resembled splotches of blood, which caught the light of his flashlight as he moved it back and forth across the patch. Something else was beyond the briars, though, perhaps a quarter mile away. At first, he thought the light might have been from his flashlight catching a damp leaf, so he flipped the switch. The small flicker in the distance remained. He stepped forward and squinted, teetering as close as he could to the patch without falling in. He could just make out smoke billowing off into the sky from a chimney in the distance, and the light appeared to be coming from a window. As the edges of a building came into focus, Oliver lost his balance and tumbled into the patch. He put his hands in front of himself and attempted to shield his face from the thorns. Instead of scraping and scratching him, though, the branches seemed to cushion his fall, bending and conforming to his body.

He lay for a moment before cautiously pushing himself up from the ground. As he regained his balance, he reached his hand out to brace himself, and his fingers brushed against something cold. At first, he recoiled but then reached out to feel for the object and figure out what he'd found. His hand worked along the object until he could make out what felt like a hand with cold and swollen fingers. He panicked and pulled away, searching frantically for his flashlight, which had fallen into the pit in front of him. The moonlight bounced off its shiny metal casing, and he scurried to reclaim it. He picked it up and turned to illuminate the scene behind him. The light from the flashlight met the glossy eyes of a body staring vacantly into the forest. The woman was ensnared in the briars, and Oliver could see deep cuts from thorns sticking into her skin. Her eyes were hazy, just as Francis's had been.

The path he had forged into the branches was gone, but without hesitation and with his heart in his throat, he ran through the thicket, past the corpse, and out into the field. The lights on the first floor of Izzy's house shone in the distance, but the place seemed quite far away. He bolted up the hill, turning what had been a fifteen-minute walk into a six-minute sprint.

CHAPTER TWELVE

"I have to admit the situation doesn't look good. The people in this town have never seen a murder before, then two mysterious deaths occur within a few weeks of your arrival. Doesn't take a detective to find that odd." Eric sat at Izzy's kitchen table and took a drink from his coffee mug. Nekko lay sprawled across the counter, eyeing the cookies Izzy had placed on the cooling rack next to her.

"I know, I know. It must look terrible, but I had nothing to do with it," Oliver replied.

At least the second body had convinced the police something more sinister was afoot than a simple heart attack, but Oliver hadn't anticipated becoming the primary suspect.

"What were you doing out by the forest tonight?" Eric asked.

Oliver wasn't sure how to answer the question. If he said he'd been out looking for the site of Nathaniel Hale's great escape, that might paint him as a loon.

"I couldn't sleep, so I decided to go on a walk. Just needed some fresh air," he replied. The statement wasn't exactly a lie, but it wasn't the whole truth either.

"Out by the forest?"

"You were looking for the briar patch, weren't you?" Izzy asked, leaning against the kitchen counter.

Oliver shot her a desperate glance, telepathically pleading for her to shut up.

"It's okay—just tell him," she said, turning toward Eric. "I showed him my paintings, you know, the ones from the art show a few years ago. He must have gone looking for the briar patch."

Oliver's face flushed.

Eric chuckled. "Oh, I remember those paintings well. So you went looking for Nathaniel's last stand?" he asked.

Oliver lowered his head in shame and nodded in affirmation.

"Anna and I found a coin in Harry's front yard when we stopped by to bring him the basket. It was sticking out of the dirt underneath the hedges, and Harry told us Martin would be able to tell us more about it." Oliver pulled the coin from his pocket and handed it to Eric. "Martin told us the story, so I thought I'd see if I could find the patch." He hoped that was enough to explain his late-night stroll to the woods.

"It wouldn't be the first time a historic town artifact popped up in a flowerbed," Eric said. "In fact, Martin makes a good chunk of money from stuff like this."

"He's already offered to buy it," Oliver added.

Eric turned the coin over in his hand. "Probably just a coincidence, but this does link both of the deaths. Don't go selling the coin yet—hold onto it for now."

He sat back in the chair and rubbed his chin. "Son, I don't think you had anything to do with this. What 'this' is, I'm not entirely sure yet, but we're going to have a look around the patch and see what we can find. Just know that even if we can clear you, I have no control over town gossip. If there's a group who thought you were guilty before, they're going to be outside with pitchforks after they find out about this."

Oliver hoped he was kidding about the pitchforks, but Eric's expression showed no signs of jest.

"Thanks for the warning," Oliver replied. "You might also want to check the house in the woods, the one on the other side of the briar patch. I saw it before I fell in, and it looked like someone was home. They may have seen something."

Eric furrowed his brow though Oliver wasn't sure why. "We'll check it out," he said. "In the meantime, it's probably best you stay put until we can release a statement and officially rule you out as a suspect. Not worried about you going anywhere—it's more for your own good than anything else."

Oliver watched from the kitchen window as the police searched the edge of the patch for several hours. Little beams of light swept across the forest floor until the team was finally able to pull the corpse free and place it on a gurney. Her face was still frozen in his mind, glossy eyed and slack-jawed, just like Francis. Unfortunately, the woman hadn't had a fleet of crows to save her, unlike Nathaniel Hale. The flashing lights from the ambulance bounced off the evening mist, as if some sort of late-night rave were happening in the field below.

Although the police had left and the night had gone quiet, Oliver wasn't going to find sleep anytime soon. He tossed and turned but couldn't rid his mind of the image of the woman whose body had lain contorted in the briars.

CHAPTER THIRTEEN

Oliver clutched his cup of coffee while Izzy stepped outside to grab the morning paper.

"Can you believe it? Her obituary is already in the paper. This town works fast," she said, returning to the kitchen and holding the newsprint at arm's length so she could read the tiny letters.

"Who was she?" Oliver asked.

"Lilly Brighton," Izzy replied.

Lilly was a widow who had lived on the outskirts of town. As luck would have it, she also lived in a cabin on the edge of the forest, although not the same one Oliver had seen beyond the tree line. Hers was another mile or two away. She had also been an active member of the Elders until her husband died a few years back.

"I didn't know her very well, but she came in for a loaf of bread every now and then and would occasionally wander up the hill for a jar of honey. Kept to herself for the most part, especially after her husband died," Izzy said.

"Another Elder?" Oliver asked. "That seems odd, doesn't it—two murders in a town that hasn't seen a murder for decades, and both victims happen to be Elders?"

Several days passed before the official cause of death was released. As with Francis, the medical examiners found that a heart attack had killed Lilly Brighton. The woman's jaw had been dislocated, exactly as Francis's had, but with no other signs of physical attack nor mysterious bruising, just a face frozen in fear. As with the other house, hers had been torn to shreds, the small one-bedroom cabin being no match for whatever force had laid waste to it. If the police hadn't found the damage, it would have appeared Lilly had simply wandered into the woods, tripped into the thorn bushes, and died. The cause of the dislocated jaw was still a mystery.

The horrifying nature of Francis's and Lilly's deaths made it impossible to direct fear at one particular thing, so the town chose to fear everything instead. Late-night meetings were canceled. A neighborhood watch was formed, and the Elders pushed the town council to implement a curfew. The local police officers beefed up patrols and brought officers from neighboring areas to assist.

Eric had been absolutely right about one thing—the town, at least the Elders, needed someone to blame. Oliver had started to attract odd looks and stares, and the neighborhood watch seemed to pass Izzy's place and the bakery several times a day. Although some in town seemed to believe Oliver's innocence, several of those with the power to make his life miserable did not. He felt watched, and the only way to avoid the feeling was to avoid the outdoors altogether.

Oliver awoke with a jolt as a flurry of pages came crashing down on his face. He'd dozed off while reading on the couch, and the corner of the hardback he'd been holding fell and hit him square in the nose. Pan lay nestled between his legs, and Nekko was busy halfheartedly hunting a fly on the windowsill.

Eric was supposed to stop by to ask some additional questions, and Oliver was eager for the visitor even if the circumstances were less than pleasant. He hadn't left the house for a few days, and he was starting to feel the walls closing in on him.

A knock at the door caught Pan by surprise, and he sprang off the couch and landed on the floor, legs sliding out from under him. The pup quickly recovered and yipped at the door.

When Oliver answered, Eric gave him a once over.

He hadn't shaved for several days, and he was wearing the clothes he'd stained with paint when decorating Izzy's station wagon for the festival. The ruined T-shirt and shorts were the only clean clothes he had left, and the layer of dirty laundry on his bedroom floor had made it look as if a floor weren't there at all.

"Still have some time to talk?" Eric asked.

Oliver nodded and led Eric to the kitchen.

"So, what can I do for you?" Oliver asked while he pulled two mugs from the cupboard and filled them at the coffee pot.

"When we spoke the other night, you mentioned a house in the woods. Where exactly did you see it?"

"Right across the briar patch where I found Lilly," Oliver replied.

"That's what I thought you said the other night. Thing is, we didn't find any houses on the other side of the patch. The entire area is vacant. It's also completely surrounded by rosebushes, and I damned near lost a liter of blood trying to cross to the other side. Ended up calling it quits. There's no way someone lives over there. Are you sure you saw a house? Could your mind have been playing tricks on you?"

"I know what I saw," he replied. "There's definitely a building on the other side of the patch." Oliver could still remember the single lit window and the smoke coming from the chimney.

"Uh-huh. We'll keep looking and let you know if we happen to find it. Aside from that, the rest of your story checks out. Lilly had been dead for some time when you found her. We still can't figure out the dislocated jaws or the gray eyes. They're a criminal signature of sorts, but we have no clue how they happened. There's still nothing to show anyone laid a finger on her. Either way, you're free and clear."

"Think you could put that on a banner and hang it in the square? I feel like I can't leave the house without being watched."

"Times might be tough now, but people have a short memory and will move on to other things inevitably. And if whatever this is continues, it'll become even more evident that you have nothing to do with it."

"You expect this to continue?" Oliver asked. "Like, more murders?"

"Lord, I hope not, but we're not ready to rule anything out. Considering the similar circumstances, I wouldn't be surprised if we see another attack. All we can do now is keep a close watch on the town and make it as difficult as possible for whoever is doing this to strike again."

A serial killer? Oliver dared not utter the words with Eric in the room. "If there's anything else I can do to help, please let me know," he said.

Eric looked down at his coffee cup and back at Oliver.

"This isn't really my business, but you look like hell, son. The best thing you can do at this point is take care of yourself."

CHAPTER FOURTEEN

Oliver watched from a safe distance as Izzy leaned over one of the beehives and pried the lid off with what appeared to be a paint scraper.

"You know, I have an extra set of clothes in the garage, if you want to help," she said. "They're pretty friendly, as bees go."

"I'll take your word for it," Oliver replied from the porch. The hives brought flashbacks to a day in the early nineties, when a bee had worked its way into his ear as he swam in his inflatable kiddy pool. He felt the tickle of the bee's tiny legs on his skin and instinctively pressed his index finger hard into his ear to relieve the itch. Fortunately, the damage was minor, but it left enough of a psychological scar to instill a deep fear of bees that kept him from straying too close to the hives.

"Oh, come on. They're docile and won't be able to

get you through the gear anyway." Izzy cocked her head to one side. "Please?" she asked.

He could practically see her puppy-dog eyes through the beekeeper's mask.

"I think Anna's calling me," he said. "Better go see what she wants." He turned and quickly walked across the porch into the kitchen. Of course, he wasn't telling the truth, but that was an effective exit strategy.

Oliver had gotten his life together over the past few days. He'd shaven, cleared the mammoth pile of laundry from his room, and had even gone outside a time or two.

Anna stood over the kitchen table, sliding one of the honeycomb frames from a vacant hive box.

"Perfect timing," she said. "Grab one of those plastic containers, and set it over there on the counter." She nodded in the direction of a small patch of vacant counter space. Oliver did as he was told and stood back as Anna placed the wooden frame longways in the container. He had never seen honeycomb up close before and knew of honey only as the amber liquid that came from bear-shaped bottles. Of course, he had a theoretical grasp on where it came from, but it was truly a beautiful thing to behold. The bees had filled the wooden frame to the edges with an intricate wax comb, using only a few thin metal wires as a foundation for the elaborate structure.

"Hand me that knife on the table over there," she said.

As far as Oliver could tell, it was just an ordinary bread knife, long with a serrated edge. He handed it to her and watched with intrigue as she gingerly cut the wax caps off of the comb, carefully running the knife down the frame. The wax sloughed off into the container below, and a few drops of golden syrup dripped off the end of the knife. She did the same for the other side before walking over to a tall metal drum in the corner of the room.

"A little help?" she asked.

Oliver followed her over to the machine and lifted the Plexiglas lid so she could slide the frame into one of the drum slots.

"So this is what you use to get all of the honey out?" he asked.

"Yep, it's like a giant centrifuge. We put the frames in here, spin it around, then open the tap at the bottom and filter the honey into a bucket."

She fit an entire box of frames into the extractor, and the centrifuge spun to life. The device reminded Oliver of a carnival ride and started to hop a bit as it picked up speed. He stepped on the bottom of the metal frame to steady it. After a few moments, Anna kicked an empty bucket underneath the spout and laid a strainer on top to filter out all the debris.

"Pull the tap," she said.

Oliver lifted the small plastic valve that kept the honey inside the drum. As he did, a thick waterfall of syrup poured into the strainer and bucket below.

"I've never seen this much honey at one time," he said. "How much do you get from each of these frames?"

"Two or three pounds," she replied.

He walked to the screen door and looked out at the hives in the yard. "You have eight hives with four boxes apiece, so that's a thousand pounds of honey? That's crazy!"

"Not quite—probably half of that, though. The lower boxes are where the queen lays all of her eggs. We don't harvest from those, plus we need to leave enough honey for the bees to eat."

"You harvest that much every year?"

"Not the first, but most of the years after that. We did have a bit of a scare with hive beetles last year, though."

"Hive beetles?"

"Yeah, they're little beetles that sneak up into the hives and lay eggs. They can ruin the stores of honey if you're not careful and can even kill entire hives. We had a little infestation, but we caught them early and made some modifications to the hives to keep them out, at least for the most part."

As he watched Izzy out in the yard, his brain couldn't help but make the connection between the bustling hives and the town. Even the smallest intruder or uninvited outsider could cause devastation to the hive if not controlled. To the town, Izzy was a hive beetle, threatening to destroy the delicate honeycomb that was the town's carefully curated aesthetic.

The harvest continued for the better part of the day, and Oliver and Anna took a break while Izzy finished up preparing the hives for winter.

No matter how hard he tried, Oliver couldn't get the house in the woods out of his head. *How could I have imagined it?* He told Izzy the story, and she confirmed no one lived on the other side of the briar patch. Oliver wanted to see for himself, and he tried to convince Anna to take a stroll with him down to the edge of the forest.

"I'm telling you now, there's nothing down there. No one lives in the woods," Anna said, trying to keep pace with him as he speed walked down the hill.

"I know, but I definitely saw something. It wasn't the wind blowing through the trees or my imagination. It was a building. It's there—I know it," he said.

They walked the tree line to the briar patch. Even though the police had hacked away at the vines to free Lilly from their tangles, the patch now looked as though it had never been touched. The blooms had faded, and he found no signs of the bright-red flowers that had speckled the patch the other night.

"So, where is this building, then?" she asked.

Oliver pointed across the brambles, edging toward the patch. He squinted, hoping to bring the building into focus once again, but he saw only trees and foliage in the distance.

She followed the path of his finger. "Nothing's there."

"I saw the house right over there." He was growing irritated and pressed up against the briars, which snagged his clothing and scraped against his arm. He pulled back, and one of the thorns left a deep scratch in his skin.

"That's odd," he said, rubbing the scratch.

"What is?" Anna asked.

"The other night, I fell right into the patch, but I didn't get a single scratch. The branches cushioned my fall. Now, they've drawn blood." As he pulled away, he noticed several small blooms on the branches that had scraped him. They appeared to be opening up before his eyes.

"I think I'm losing my mind. Do you see those?" he asked, pointing at the blooms. "Those flowers weren't there a minute ago."

Anna shrugged.

They walked along the tree line in the direction of

Lilly's house, which sat next to the woods a mile or so down the field. When they arrived at the tiny cottage, the door was still cordoned off with police tape.

"Apparently, the inside was torn apart, just like Francis's place," he said.

"You think whoever destroyed the house dumped her in the patch?" Anna asked.

"That or she ran for her life and got tangled up— doesn't explain the jaw, though."

"That's terrifying," she said, rubbing her arms for warmth.

Oliver stared at the entryway to the cottage. The door was constructed of several vertical planks of sturdy wood, with two crossbeams to hold it together. He stepped forward and examined a crack that ran down one of the center boards.

"Whatever was after Francis nearly broke her door in two. This one's just as bad," he said.

He noticed a small scratch at the bottom of the door and knelt down to get a better look. A crude S shape was carved into the wood in red ink.

"Come here and look at this," he said, beckoning Anna over to the door. "Have you seen anything like this before?"

She knelt down next to him and examined the carving.

"No, what do you think it is?" she asked.

"It's a symbol of some kind. Doesn't look like it's supposed to be there, though. Look at the splinters. It's like someone carved it in with a knife," Oliver said. "But there's some kind of ink too." He stepped back from the doorway. "Do you think...?"

"Think what?"

"The person who attacked Lilly carved it? It's crazy, but I wonder if this could have been carved into the other door as well," he said.

"There's only one way to find out," she replied. "And we won't even need to bother Harry to do it."

If the pattern had been carved into Francis's door, the police could have easily overlooked it because of the bright-red paint.

Anna and Oliver reached Francis's home half an hour later after crossing the field and making their way back into town and through the alley next to the bakery. But something was different about the house— the bright-red door had been replaced.

Without hesitation, Oliver marched up the walkway and knocked on the door.

"What are you doing?" she asked. "Don't bother him."

But it was too late. Harry answered the door, a bit more composed this time and fully dressed.

"Oliver. What brings you here?" he asked.

"We were wondering if you still have the red door,"

he said.

Anna rubbed her forehead in embarrassment.

"Um, well, I was going to get rid of it but couldn't bring myself to do it. Why do you ask?"

"I don't mean to intrude, but is there any chance we could take a look?" he asked. "Just wanted to check something."

Harry seemed puzzled. "Uh, sure, I guess," he said. "Come on in." He opened the door wider and gestured inside.

As they turned the corner into the dining room, the bright-red door waited for them. Harry had converted it into a kitchen table and filled the gaps where the door had cracked with a shiny resin.

"What do you think?" he asked. "I'm not much of a craftsman, but I think it turned out all right."

"It's beautiful," Anna said, choking up a bit.

The piece served as an elegant memorial to Harry's late wife.

"I know it's just a door, but she loved the damn thing for some reason. I had to save it. Now it feels like I still get to eat every meal with her," he said.

Oliver walked around to the other side of the table. He traced his finger along another crudely carved S pattern on the bottom right side.

"The scratches are here too," he said. "Harry, did you see this?"

Harry walked toward him and looked down at the table. He scratched at the carving with his fingernail. "Oh, that. Figured it was just a scratch."

"This is the same pattern that was carved into Lilly Brighton's door," Oliver said.

Harry immediately pulled his hand back, as if the door had bitten him. "What?"

"We found this on Lilly's door—the same exact pattern. We've got to tell the police. The red ink blends right in with the color of the door, so I missed it the first time around."

Harry's face turned ashen, and he stared off into space for several moments before regaining composure. "I think it's best if you leave now," he said.

"Wait—why?" Oliver asked.

"Francis is gone. None of this will bring her back. I've already talked to the police and told them everything I know."

"But this is new. Eric never mentioned this. People are being murdered, and whoever's doing it might very well do it again," he said, pleading for Harry's cooperation.

"Tell the police if you want, but I don't want any part of it. Now, please leave," Harry pointed toward the door.

"Harry, we're sorry," Anna chimed in. "We'll go." She shot a stern glance at Oliver.

He reluctantly agreed, and Harry led the two to the front door.

"What's wrong with you?" she asked, once safely out of earshot.

"What do you mean? We found a pattern that could help the police figure all this out," he said.

"I know. But you can't just barge into someone's house who's just lost his wife and dredge all this stuff back up. We'll tell Eric. That's fine, but show a little compassion, for God's sake." Her face was turning a shade of red that reminded Oliver of Francis's door. She wasn't quite yelling, but her voice was only a few decibels away.

"You're right," he said. "I'm sorry, but this could help the police prevent another murder. Maybe the symbol means something, and they could tie it to the killer."

The police had indeed missed the carved symbols in the original investigation. Aside from dusting the door handles for prints, they'd had no reason to inspect the door that closely. But the discovery didn't move the case forward. Despite a thorough search, they were unable to determine the meaning of the symbol or where it might have come from. Even Martin, who had been so helpful with the coin, didn't recognize the obscure etching. The find appeared to lead to nothing more than a dead end.

CHAPTER FIFTEEN

Oliver lay on his back in the sunroom. The bright sunlight warmed his body and helped him to momentarily forget how dark his world had become. He twisted the coin in his hand, allowing the sunlight to flash across its metal surface. Pan lay next to him and appeared to be wondering whether or not the object in Oliver's hand was edible. Izzy was out tending to the bees, so Oliver was keeping an eye on the mischievous pup since he clearly had no other place to be for the foreseeable future.

Exiled.

The word hung over him like a personal rain cloud. Almost a week had passed since Anna burst through the bakery doors in a redheaded rage. Her father had overheard a conversation among Madeline and a few of the Elders concerning their options for forcing Oliver's exit from Christchurch. "Exile" was the term Anna used. Apparently, several in the town didn't care Oliver had been cleared by the police. He was guilty in their minds.

Fortunately, exiles had gone out of style with witchcraft trials. Still—the idea that some in the town wanted him to leave so badly they'd propose forcibly removing him made him question why he continued to stay. Several days had passed since Izzy had kindly given him the week off to mope around the house. The neighborhood watch took frequent strolls by Izzy's place, so Oliver resumed his hermitage. Things were a mess, and his presence was only making the relationship between Izzy and the Elders worse, despite her constant reassurance to the contrary. But something in him told him to stay—told him he could help find the person who was leaving bodies scattered around Christchurch.

The back door creaked, and Izzy came in with her beekeeper mask in hand. When she saw Oliver sprawled on the floor, she set her mask down on the coffee table and lay next to him.

"What's on your mind, kiddo?" she asked.

"Nothing, just warming up in the sun a bit," he replied.

"You've barely moved all week. I'd say you should be sufficiently warm by now, don't you think?"

"It hasn't been a week," he replied. "Okay, well maybe a business week," he corrected himself. "What's the point in going outside if everyone out there wants you gone?"

"Welcome to my world, bud, but it's not everyone. I've lived in this town for most of my life, and there are plenty of people here who still want nothing to do with me." Izzy paused. "But I'll let you in on a little secret. I don't do things for them—I do things for me. Even though some in this town would prefer it if I lived somewhere else—the side of a remote mountain, perhaps—there are still some great people here. It's a beautiful place to live, and I'd never be able to find another place with this much land and these gorgeous views. So, I stay for me. Sometimes, you just have to do things others aren't going to agree with if those are the things that make you happy."

"I can feel them all staring at me, hating me from a distance. I know I didn't do anything wrong, but I feel so guilty."

"Oliver, why did you walk away from your job?" She turned her head to face him.

"I had no choice. I couldn't afford to waste away doing something that I hated. I couldn't afford to sit behind a desk for the rest of my life," he replied.

"If that's the case, can you afford to waste away on the sunroom floor? You'd be better off back in the city than here on the ground." She pecked him on the side of his head then stood up and went into the kitchen to start dinner.

He lay on the floor for several more minutes before tucking the coin into his pocket, hopping up, and walking to the kitchen to grab his coat. Izzy stood over a large pot of beans she'd been soaking since morning. He said nothing but walked over and wrapped his arms around her.

"You're right," he said. "I'm going to go out for a bit."

"I'll leave you some leftovers if you're not back for dinner. Have fun," she said, patting his back.

"Oh, and I'm going to borrow the bike," he added.

Izzy's bike matched the color of her car, at least its color before they'd painted it for the festival. Several years had passed since he had last ridden a bike, and the ape-hanger handlebars didn't make riding any easier, so he wobbled a bit on the gravel before gaining his balance.

His face parted the chilly night air as he flew past the vibrant trees, whose leaves matched the color of the sunset. Fall was in full swing, and soon the town would be filled with pumpkins and trick-or-treaters. The owner of the marketplace was pulling in barrels and crates of produce for the evening as Oliver whizzed by, receiving a nasty glare from a group of neighborhood watchers who stood next to the founder's statue.

Anna lived on the other side of town, a ways back behind the bakery, in a small cottage overlooking the lake. Oliver had helped her take a few boxes of honey home a few days before, and the place was hard to miss. The window trim was painted bright orange, and the entire building seemed to be sculpted out of curved wooden shingles. Handmade stained glass filled one of the front windows.

Oliver hopped off the bike and knocked on the door. Anna greeted him, wearing an apron and covered in flour.

"You know the bakery's closed, right?" he asked.

"What are you doing here?"

"Just been holed up in the house for a few days and thought I'd get some fresh air. Thought maybe you could use some too."

"Absolutely! Come on in." She ushered him in through the arched doorway.

The tiny cottage was just as eclectic on the inside as on the outside. The light through the stained glass cast a brilliant aura over the living room, and the kitchen's large picture window, located just above the sink, provided a spectacular view of the lake.

The kitchen was filled with stacks of bakeware containers scattered across the counters. A leaning tower of bread teetered in one of the corners.

"I know, the baking's a bit out of control," she said.

"You think?"

"Baking's always been a stress reliever for me."

"You must be in the middle of a mental breakdown, then," he said, observing the carbohydrate landscape.

"Feel free to take whatever you'd like. I've been meaning to bring some over to the house, and we're going to take the rest up to the farmer's market this weekend." Anna untied her apron, folded it, and set it on top of one of the cookie boxes since no other clear surfaces were left.

"Come out for a drink with me," he said.

"What? Are you crazy? I wouldn't be caught dead out in this town. They've been nothing but terrible to you, terrible to Izzy," she said.

"Come on. Screw the town. It's just a few bad apples, anyway. Let's go out and have some fun. You're stress baking, for God's sake!"

Anna thought for a moment. "Oh, what the hell. Let's go!"

Oliver waited in the living room while Anna washed up. Her kitchen library consisted of dozens of cookbooks, mostly of the baking variety, but her living room shelves were filled with travel books. His eyes scanned the spines: Mykonos, Ireland, Amsterdam, and tons of others.

"Ready?" she asked, catching him by surprise. She had changed out of her floured clothing, washed her face, and thrown her hair up into a bun.

Once outside, they both stood in front of the bike. "Shall we walk, or should we put my balance to the test?" he asked.

Anna looked down at the banana seat. "I'm up for an adventure," she replied.

He had been somewhat joking and was caught off guard by her willingness to so freely put her life in his hands. "All right, let's do it."

Oliver sat on the bike and steadied it so that Anna could climb on behind him. She put her hands around his waist and her feet up on the wheel frame, then he pushed off, hoping he could keep the bike steady until he reached full speed. The first few feet were a bit turbulent, but Oliver actually found it easier to keep the bike balanced with Anna than without.

"You're a natural. Been taking a lot of girls around on bicycle rides lately?" she asked.

"Only bakers," he replied.

They arrived at The Horseman without incident although Oliver figured the ride back home might be a bit more difficult, depending on how many pints their visit to the tavern entailed.

He could hear the chatter of the pubgoers from outside, and a police car sat watch nearby. The car seemed extremely out of place for the small town. Sometimes Oliver forgot he was living in the twenty-first century, with all the preserved history around him, but the cruiser reminded him that even small towns weren't immune to the terrors of the modern-day world.

"Kind of weird to have all of these cops around," Anna said. "Feels like we have to be on our best behavior even though I know we aren't doing anything wrong."

"At least we know there are people looking out for us," he said, waving to the officer in the cruiser. The officer rested his hand on the side of the car and gave a halfhearted wave in return. Oliver didn't recognize him as one of the Christchurch police, who were easy to spot, considering the town had only three of them.

Oliver held the door of the tavern open for Anna. The pub was alive with the hum of the local townsfolk —at least until they walked in. The buzz died down to a murmur at the first sight of Oliver. Several sets of eyes followed the two as they made their way to the bar although the bartender seemed oblivious to the sudden lull in conversation.

"Anna! Good to see you. What can I get you two?" he asked.

Oliver ordered a wheat beer and Anna a stout.

"Didn't know you liked dark beer," Oliver said, pulling out his wallet.

"Why wouldn't I? It's because I'm a woman, isn't it?" she asked, feigning offense.

The pub clientele eventually lost interest and returned to their drunken conversations.

"Is the roof open?" she asked the bartender. "It's a bit of a tough crowd tonight—might be nice to have some privacy."

"Always open for you, dear, but you might freeze out there. It's pretty chilly outside," he replied. "And if anybody catches you, you know the deal. You're not allowed up there, and you were trespassing." He smiled at Anna.

She grabbed Oliver by the arm as the bartender set their drinks in front of him.

"Come on. I want to show you something." She pulled him to the staircase next to the bar, and they climbed the steps. Golden numbers were painted on each of the guest-room doors lining the hallway. The fact that this was the only inn, motel, or hotel in town still baffled him, especially since the place had only four rooms. Anna walked to the end of the hallway and turned toward a small broom closet.

"Hold this," she said, handing Oliver her beer and opening the closet door.

The closet held a set of brooms and a mop bucket but also had a metal ladder bolted to the back wall of it. Anna put her foot on the first rung and carefully climbed. She unlatched the hatch at the top of the ladder, pulled herself up to the roof, then reached down to grab the beers from Oliver.

"Come on up," she said.

He closed the closet door behind himself and began the short climb to the roof. As he looked up through the hatch, the brilliant night sky came into view. The countless stars and planets were overwhelming. He could likely see these same stars from the ground, but he simply hadn't bothered to look. *How could I have missed them?* The light was different in the small town. He was lucky to see a bright planet every now and then from his studio apartment, but Christchurch was free from the bright lights that polluted the atmosphere in the city.

The roof was clearly not meant for patrons, but someone had nailed a wooden bench down and built a small decorative fence around the edges. It certainly wouldn't prevent any accidental falls onto the stone patio below and was more of a decoration than anything else.

Anna stood at the edge and looked off into the

distance. The entire town was visible from the rooftop. Oliver could see the town square and could even make out Anna's cottage in the distance. He turned around and saw Izzy's house, with a single light shining from the second floor. He imagined she had taken dinner up to her studio and was hard at work on her next subversive masterpiece. The forest sat in the valley below, and a few speckled lights shone through the trees.

"Look over here," he said.

"Huh?" Anna replied, walking over next to him.

"Don't you see those lights off in the distance?" he asked.

Anna squinted.

"I don't see anything," she replied.

"They're in the trees, right where I found the body. It's where I brought you that day and where I saw the house the night I found Lilly."

"Maybe it's just a bunch of campers or hunters or something. The police could be taking another look in the woods," she said. Her answer was rational, but it still didn't explain what he'd seen in the woods several nights before. No matter how hard he tried, he just wasn't able to rid his mind of it.

Oliver stood in silence for a moment.

"You know, at some point, you're going to have to let it go," she said, as if reading his thoughts.

"Let what go?" he asked, feigning ignorance.

"Lilly, Francis, this whole thing. If anyone's going to figure things out, the police will. You shouldn't lose sleep over it. We have to keep living our lives. If not, we're just as bad as the Elders."

Oliver wasn't sure how he would be able to "let it go." He'd found two bodies within a matter of weeks.

"So you like to travel? I noticed all of the books on your shelf," he said, doing his best to change the subject although the transition was somewhat jarring.

"I wish," she replied. "I went to Canada once, but that's about it."

"I'm surprised the daughter of the mayor hasn't traveled the world. What about college? Didn't do any traveling then?"

"Didn't go, actually," she replied. "I started working in the bakery after high school. That decision certainly didn't go over well with *the mayor*. College just wasn't for me. I do wish I had the chance to see a bit more of the world, though."

"There's still plenty of time," he replied.

She grinned as if distracted by another thought. "Come over here and look at this." She took him by the hand and pulled him back to the other side of the roof. "See over there?" She pointed.

"You mean your cottage?" he asked.

"No, the lake," she replied, "just on the other side."

"What about it?"

"Sometimes I look out of the kitchen window or sit out back and watch the water and imagine I'm somewhere else. The water looks the same everywhere, you know? It could be a lake in Europe or Australia. Occasionally, I can even convince myself that I'm not in Christchurch anymore. Been doing that a lot lately, kinda wishing I could get away for a while."

"Why don't you?" he asked.

"I can't just leave Izzy. She needs my help."

"Well, I'm here. I can help," he said, somewhat offended.

"Yeah, but Izzy was willing to take a chance on me when I had no practical experience. She helped me find the cottage when I didn't want to mooch off Dad anymore, and she even called in a few favors to have it fixed on the cheap so I could afford it. I owe her a lot. And you don't even know how long you're going to be here. You're still planning to go back, right? Back to the city?"

"I guess so," he replied. He had thought a lot about *going back* in the last week. He'd have to go back at some point, find a job, and move on with his life. Eventually, he would run out of money, and he was relatively certain his landlord had grown accustomed to being paid rent. He couldn't stay in Christchurch forever. Still, something was holding him here. The murders were a part of it—he wanted to clear his name, to find out who had been terrorizing the town and leaving bodies strewn about for him to discover like gruesome Easter eggs. He was also growing attached to Izzy and Anna. They'd been a big part of his life recently and had accepted him for who he was. Nights like these made him want to stay.

CHAPTER SIXTEEN

Anna held on tightly to Oliver's waist as the bike wobbled down the gravel path toward the cottage. The night had gotten colder, and the breeze seemed to cut through Oliver's skin and into his bones. He dropped her off at the cottage doorstep and waited until she was safely inside to turn his bike around and head back to Izzy's. With the two recent attacks fresh in his mind, he worried about her living in solitude on the edge of town. Breaking into the tiny cottage wouldn't take much. Fortunately, Anna seemed capable of defending herself, based on her aggressive dough-kneading techniques.

The bike tires hummed against the street as Oliver made his way to the other side of town and down the dirt road next to the market. But instead of turning in for the night, he stopped by Izzy's house to grab a flashlight then flew down the hill to the open field. He set his sights on the briar patch at the edge of the forest and toward the mysterious lights he had seen earlier from the roof of the tavern. He couldn't rid himself of the thought something was waiting for him on the other side of the patch.

He parked the bike at the edge of the forest and approached the patch. He reached his hand out to grab one of the thorny vines, fueled by the liquid courage from the pub. The other day, the thorns had pricked and scratched his arms, and he ran his finger over one of the thorns, expecting the same. Instead, the thorn folded flat under his touch. He took a small step forward, putting one foot into the vines. The briars crunched under his feet but did not scratch him and seemed to shift out of his way as he stepped deeper into the patch. These couldn't have been the same vines that had tangled around Lilly's body—these appeared to clear a path for him as he crossed to the other side.

The house came into focus in the distance. No light emanated from the window, but he could still make out the edges of the stone structure. *I knew it had to be here.* As he approached, he identified the source of the light he'd seen from the roof of the tavern. The row of dotted lights was in fact a trail of gas street lamps, which lined the cobblestone walkway ahead. *But why couldn't anyone else see them?* Everyone with whom he had spoken had been certain no one lived on the other side of the briar patch, but he was coming face-to-face with proof. These structures were old, and he found it odd that they had gone unnoticed.

Were the police hiding something? Why would they lie about being able to see the house?

The mysterious building in the distance was, in fact, a house after all. Oliver followed the path of streetlights past the simple stone two-story home. The illuminated walkway led him into a square of sorts, not unlike the one in Christchurch. Like the town on the other side of the patch, this one had a memorial statue in the center as well. The figure stood, reaching toward the heavens, its body wrapped in vines and being pulled down toward the earth. He read the metal plaque on the base of the statue.

For our glorious leader.

Dedicated by the Briarwood town council.

BRIARWOOD?

The plaque also had a seal imprinted next to the dedication. Oliver pulled the coin from his pocket and held it next to the image. Both showed a crow entangled by briars.

The coin belongs to Briarwood.

The square was bordered by shops and buildings of various sizes, and all sat in darkness, aside from a large building in the corner of the square. As he walked toward the lit building, he noticed the complete absence of power lines or cars parked along the streets. Christchurch had a historic charm, but this place appeared to be frozen in time completely. The large structure appeared to be a town hall but was oddly proportioned. Instead of taking up a large section of the square, like the one in Christchurch, the stone building seemed to have been built upward instead of out.

The hall must have had four to five floors, and an odd metal turret jutted from the top. The turret's ornate base held up walls made completely from glass. Corroded spirals of copper wrapped around the panes and formed a filigreed cap, and light radiated from the room as if it were a humongous lantern. The building was the tallest in the square by far and seemed to be almost impossibly constructed.

Chatter echoed from the first floor of the building, while the rest of the town sat in silence. He sneaked to the side of the structure and climbed up on a bench, which sat near an open window. He struggled to lift himself up and peer inside.

The hall was lined with long wooden benches, and all had been filled to capacity. The scene reminded him of his first town-hall meeting, which brought feelings of anxiety rushing back to him. Light came from gas wall sconces lining the room and cast an eerie flickering glow on the crowd. The people were very strangely dressed, with a hodgepodge of Victorian-era fashion accented with decorative touches that were oddly out of place.

A large opera box extended from the front of the room, in which sat an elaborately carved wooden desk and a thronelike gilded chair. The box was suspended by ornate iron beams bridged by two giant circular pieces resembling spoked bicycle wheels on either side. He wasn't sure who typically occupied the chair, but he or she was clearly someone of great importance. The seat was vacant though, and the crowd seemed to be ignoring the man who stood underneath, waving his arms frantically and vying for their attention. Eventually, enough of those in the room noticed his desperate pleas, and the room began to quiet.

"Please, please!" the man shouted. "Let us bring this meeting to order." He clearly wasn't the one who belonged in the throne and seemed nervous to stand alone in front of the room of raucous townsfolk. This man was a stand-in.

"Where is our glorious leader?" A voice emerged from the crowd.

"As I told you before, our glorious leader hath fallen ill and is recovering at home. He should be fully recovered any day now," the man replied.

Glorious leader?

The peculiar language and fashion made Oliver feel as if he'd stumbled into a mediocre renaissance fair.

"You are a liar. No one has seen him for weeks," another townsperson shouted, identity safely obscured by the large crowd. "He is gone, and you know it!"

"Now, I would hate to tell our glorious leader that certain members of our town are showing their disobedience by questioning my honesty." It sounded like a threat but was made less menacing by the wavering tone of the man's voice.

A woman, perhaps midthirties, stood in a middle row of seats.

"Now listen here, little weasel, you can threaten us all day, but we all know that he's gone. And threats won't do much good if we're all dead by the time he gets back."

The crowd cheered in agreement.

"No one is going to die. Measures are in place to

ensure the town is protected. The barrier has held for centuries, and it's not going anywhere anytime soon. Might I add: those protections are all in place thanks to the royal family. Our glorious leader continues to protect us from all outsiders who are waiting to do us harm, and the least we can do is show our—"

Oliver felt a hand wrap around his leg and yank him down from the window ledge.

"Can I help you?" the man asked. His broad-shouldered frame was imposing, and he wore an armband with the Briarwood seal stitched into the cloth.

Oliver panicked. "Just passing through. I was just on my way out—"

"Haven't seen you in town before. Where do you live?" The man interrupted.

"Just on the other side of the briar patch, actually."

The man's eyebrows furrowed. He grabbed Oliver by the collar of his shirt and lifted him up against the stone wall.

"Came to spy on us, eh? Why are you here? How did you cross?" he shouted.

"I-I swear, I was walking through the briars and stumbled upon this place. I can just turn around and go home. I'll leave, I promise."

"No one crosses the briars. What is your wicked purpose?"

In a moment of panic, Oliver flipped his flashlight

on in the man's face. The man released his grip and stumbled backward, disoriented by the sudden burst of light. Oliver fell to the ground and regained his footing. As the man lunged toward him, Oliver ran for the edge of town and the promise of safety awaiting him on the other side of the briar patch.

The man let out an angry growl, which escaped through clenched teeth. "Come back here!" he yelled, and his footsteps quickly followed.

Oliver ran past the streetlights and the dark stone building and into the depths of the forest.

As he sprinted into the briar patch, Oliver heard the footsteps stop suddenly behind him. He jogged through the brambles, which seemed to glide out of his way. He still couldn't believe that the tangled mess, which had wrapped Lilly in a death grip, moved so easily for him. *Why?*

Once at a safe distance, he turned back toward the mysterious town and the man who had given him chase. The lumbering figure stood in amazement on the other side of the patch as if he were a dog constrained by an electric fence. "Stay out of here," he yelled, pacing back and forth along the edge of the patch. After a few moments, he rubbed his head and ran back toward Briarwood.

He's getting reinforcements. Oliver took one final look at the town and turned toward Izzy's house and the promise of safety awaiting him at the top of the hill. When he turned though, he was startled by a mysterious shape standing in his path. He lifted the flashlight to illuminate the figure, revealing the slender silhouette of a woman. She was perhaps his age or slightly younger and wore a tattered white nightdress. He stood for a moment, puzzled by her sudden appearance, and waited for her to say something. She stood unflinching in the moonlight.

"You scared the crap out of me," he said. "Are you all right?"

The figure didn't move. Her long hair covered her face in a tangled sea of black.

"Can you hear me? Are you okay?" he repeated, slowly stepping toward her.

Oliver noticed she wasn't wearing any shoes, and he didn't recognize her from town. She stood, slightly swaying, with knobby knees turned inward and shoulders back so far that her arms hung limp behind her.

The figure tilted her head to one side, just as Pan did when he was trying to understand Izzy's commands. As Oliver came within a foot or two of her, she hobbled backward.

"It's okay. I'm trying to help you," he said. "What happened to you?"

The woman slowly raised an arm, and her fingers hung limply from her hand. Her fingernails were long, chipped, and dirty, as if she had been clawing at the earth. At first, she stood, arm raised in his direction, but then she pulsed her fingers at Oliver as if flicking water droplets from her fingertips. His flashlight flickered and died, and he quickly realized the woman wasn't the one in need of help after all. He frantically smacked the flashlight until it sputtered back to life, but the woman had vanished, leaving an unobscured path back to Izzy's house.

The woods slowly receded into the distance as he looked over his shoulder to ensure he wasn't being followed. He pedaled as quickly as he could up the steep hill to Izzy's place. He could see the light from her studio in the distance and longed for the safety of the canary-yellow structure sitting just up the hill.

Izzy must have heard the door slam from her studio and came downstairs to see what all the commotion was about.

"Everything all right?" she asked, descending the staircase, with Pan tumbling down behind her.

Oliver fought to regain his breath. "Yeah," he lied. "Just came back from a little ride."

"You've been gone for hours."

"Just stopped by Anna's and went to the tavern for a bit." He left out the part about the forest—those details could wait.

He wasn't sure what he had just stumbled into but

didn't want to give Izzy another reason to be afraid. The townspeople were in a panic, and adding a ghost girl to the mix would do little to help. *But who was she?*

Later that night, Nekko lay nestled in the crook of Oliver's arm while he struggled to fall asleep.

No one lives in the woods. He thought back to what he had been told several times before. Oliver was certain he had taken Anna to the same spot—he knew it—but they weren't able to see any of the things that had been so apparent tonight. *Why could I walk through the briars without a scratch tonight but not earlier? What was different?*

Day and night.

Oliver had been able to see the lights and building at the edge of Briarwood only at night, and the briars scratched him only during the day. But this didn't explain why the police had such a difficult time removing the body, nor why Anna couldn't see the lights from the rooftop of the tavern. Only Oliver had been able to see them.

He felt the outline of the coin through his jean fabric and slid it from his pocket. The coin hadn't been with him the other day when he brought Anna to the edge of the woods. He ran his thumb over the etching of the crow. It had been with him tonight and the other night when he found the body. Perhaps the coin had somehow given him access to all that lay on the other side of the briar patch and protected him from the thorns. The guard was unable to chase him through the briars. *No one crosses the briars.* The guard had said it himself, but the coin must have somehow allowed him to do so. The idea was a crazy one, but he was beginning to think the coin was a key to Briarwood.

After several deep-breathing sessions and a few hours of tossing and turning, Oliver finally fell into a paranoid dream. The briars held him close to the ground, confining his limbs and preventing movement. He struggled to free himself, but their grip was too tight, and he was too weak to rip the curled branches from the earth. Eventually, they melted away, and he was lying in his own bed yet still unable to move. A figure stood over him. With his eyes half open, he could make out the stringy black hair of the girl from the field. But the hair had fallen away from her face as she leaned over him, revealing a jagged, yellowed smile that glistened in the moonlight. She reached toward him, but Oliver jolted awake just as her fingernail grazed his cheek.

He sat up and looked around the room, which was empty, aside from his large perturbed tabby.

CHAPTER SEVENTEEN

The metal bell jingled against the door, an unusual sound for the late-morning lull, when most of the display cases had been picked clean. Oliver peered out into the empty bakery as a man crossed the storefront and sat in one of the booths. He was oddly dressed, with a blue suit and matching top hat that reminded Oliver of a circus ringmaster's uniform. His clothes were certainly vintage, but Oliver had a hard time telling from which century they came. The man's curled mustache had been meticulously waxed to perfect symmetry.

"Think you have a friend who needs a coffee," Izzy said, sitting at the large metal table and looking up from a stack of papers.

Oliver stepped into the front of the shop and brought a coffee pot over to the man.

"Coffee?" he asked.

"I'd love a cup," the man replied.

Oliver filled the empty cup at the table. He set the pot on the warmer behind the counter and returned to take the man's order. "Anything else for you today?" he asked.

"Actually, just you, if you don't mind," he replied.

Oliver thought he had misheard. "I'm sorry—what was that?"

"Just a moment of your time. It looks like you may have a few minutes to spare," the man said, looking around the empty storefront. "Sit with me. I'll be brief."

The request was unusual, but Oliver obliged. He sat across from the man and folded his hands on the table. "What's on your mind?" he asked.

"I believe you may have something that belongs to me," he said, taking a sip of his coffee.

"Not sure what you mean," Oliver replied.

"I hear that you stumbled upon a coin." He looked up at Oliver. "You see, I had a coin stolen from me a few weeks ago, one with a little crow on it. It was a cherished family heirloom, something that's been passed down for centuries, and I'd like to have it back."

Oliver scrambled to think of a response. He couldn't just hand over the coin, especially given last night's peculiar adventure. *Who is this guy anyway?*

"I wish I could help, but I handed it over to the police," he lied. "I'm sure they'd be happy to talk to you about it, though."

Oliver noticed a flicker of contempt in the man's eyes.

"Son, hasn't anyone told you it's not polite to lie?"

"I'm sorry, sir, but I'm not lying," Oliver said, bristling. "You know, the coin was found at the scene of a murder, so whoever left it there may have had something to do with it. You really should speak to the police. They may have some questions for you too. If it was stolen, perhaps you could identify the person who stole it."

The man raised his voice. "I really don't have time for this nonsense. Now, if you just hand over the coin, I'll be on my way."

Oliver squirmed in his seat. "I wish I could help, but I don't have it. You should talk to the police, though. Don't you want to help catch a murderer?"

The man stood up.

"Well, I can see you're a busy man, so I'll let you return to your work." He gestured toward the empty booths.

"I didn't catch your name," Oliver said.

"You'll know it soon enough," the man replied as he walked toward the bakery door. He carried an elaborate cane although he didn't seem to need it. When he reached the door, he used the cane's metal tip to push it open.

Oliver, who had been holding his breath, let out a deep exhalation. He wasn't sure what to do. If he called Eric, the police might take the coin from him. He wouldn't be able to get to the bottom of what was happening if he couldn't get back to Briarwood.

When Oliver walked into the kitchen, he noticed Izzy standing against the door frame, clutching a baseball bat.

"What's that for?" he asked.

"It looked like he was hassling you," she replied. "Can never be too careful. Just wanted to be ready in case things went south."

"Since when do you keep a bat back here?"

"Since Francis was murdered in the alley next to my store." She pointed with the bat.

"Fair enough." Oliver found it difficult to imagine Izzy fighting off an intruder or belligerent customer, but he had no problem believing she would try.

He poured a cup of coffee for himself and sat at the kitchen table for a few minutes, trying to get his heart rate under control. As he calmed himself, an obvious realization washed over him. The man knew about the coin, knew about its history, and somehow knew Oliver possessed it. If it was truly a family heirloom, then the man must have known about Briarwood as well. *Could he be the glorious leader?*

CHAPTER EIGHTEEN

J ack-o'-lanterns lined the path to Anna's cottage, which had been decked out in cobwebs and a mishmash of Halloween flare.

Izzy had impressed the importance of Halloween in Christchurch to Oliver several times that week leading up to the holiday, and he found it surprising that a woman who often railed against town tradition was so eager to participate in this one. Unfortunately, Izzy's place was too far off the beaten path for trick-or-treaters, so she and Oliver packed decorations into the station wagon and made a few trips back and forth to Anna's cottage. Izzy had spent the better part of a week carving pumpkins, and Oliver had even created a few wooden caricatures for the yard.

The animals weren't safe from the festivities either. Inside, Izzy had somehow managed to strap a small witch's hat to Nekko's head with an attached cape, and Nekko was now hiding under Anna's living room sofa. Pan had gotten off easy with a Frankenstein-bolt collar.

Izzy finished putting on her costume in Anna's restroom and emerged wearing a brightly colored dress with a layer of white embroidered cotton underneath. The grease-painted unibrow was a giveaway

"Frida Kahlo?" Oliver asked.

"Yeah, and what the hell are you?" she replied.

Oliver straightened his black wig, which came to a swirl-like tip, as if he were wearing a headful of black soft serve. He held up his bladed hands, which he'd fashioned out of cut cardboard, old woolen gloves, and a copious amount of hot glue.

Izzy shrugged her shoulders.

"Edward Scissorhands. You know, from the movie," he said. A sketch of the character adorned Oliver's apartment wall.

"What movie?"

"Um, *Edward Scissorhands*."

"I don't go to the movies much anymore."

"It came out thirty years ago."

"I've been busy."

Oliver rolled his eyes and started to speak, but Anna caught his attention, emerging from the closet with a large brown paper bag.

"Whatcha got there?" he asked.

Anna walked to one of the empty glass bowls by the door and poured in the contents of the bag. Full-size candy bars tumbled into the bowl until they reached the brim. Between Anna's bag of candy and the stash Izzy had picked up at the store, they had enough to feed several towns' worth of kids.

"You really go through all of this candy?" he asked.

"Every year," Anna replied.

"What about your costume? What are you dressed as?"

"An angry baker who has to get up at four tomorrow morning." She smirked.

Miniature cowboys, zombies, and princesses came out in droves, and not just the children from Christchurch but many from neighboring towns as well. After an hour and a half, the cottage's candy stash had dwindled to half a bowl's worth. As the steady stream of trick-or-treaters slowed to a trickle, Izzy took charge of candy-distribution duties.

"Why don't you two take a walk to the square?" she asked.

Anna looked at her watch. "I could go for some fresh air."

"What's in the square?" Oliver asked.

"Some of the old geezers set up a few card tables and let everyone sample the cider they've been brewing throughout the year. A few cups of that stuff, and you'll be three sheets to the wind." She laughed.

Several police cruisers still lingered on the borders of town, but the past week or two had been quiet, and the community seemed to have taken a collective sigh of relief. Perhaps whoever had been terrorizing Christchurch had simply moved on, and the hum of little voices, decorations, and autumn sounds seemed to overpower any lingering nervousness. As for the man in the blue suit who'd wandered into the bakery, Oliver hadn't seen him since. He debated whether or not to tell Eric about the encounter but decided against it. Cryptic threats weren't against the law, and telling Eric would likely involve surrendering the coin, which he kept safely tucked away behind a loose wooden baseboard in his room.

The people in the houses on the street had gradually started to dim the lights, a message to the remaining trick-or-treaters that they were closed for business. Oliver could hear the buzz coming from the square as he and Anna rounded the street leading into it.

The sound of shattering glass and a bloodcurdling scream filled the night air, momentarily drowning out the town merriment and shuffling autumn trees. Anna and Oliver turned around, searching for the source of the sound. As they ran toward the commotion, heads peered out from behind curtains, and a few townsfolk appeared on their doorsteps. By the time the two had arrived at Madeline's front lawn, just a few streets away, a small crowd had gathered in the grass.

"Ma'am. Ma'am, can you hear me?" An officer stood over Madeline, who lay sprawled on the ground. He leaned down next to her and checked her pulse.

Madeline came to and let out a soft groan. She lifted her head, and a look of fear washed over her when she saw the crowd forming around her. "Oh God! I'm only in a bathrobe," she slurred. As she began to lift her right arm to tug her gown closed, she winced and clutched her elbow.

"Hey, hey," the officer said, "just lie still. Help is on the way, and you're going to be fine." He pulled the robe tight around her waist then covered her with his jacket.

The old leaded window on Madeline's second floor had been blown apart, with glass scattered everywhere on the ground below.

"She must have fallen out of the window onto the transom and rolled into the bushes," Oliver said.

Although the window had been destroyed—frame completely ripped from the house—he saw no other signs of an explosion or fire, and the rest of the building appeared to be perfectly fine from the outside.

The officer was quickly joined by another, who came running across the lawn.

Madeline looked up at them and began to cry. "I was attacked," she said. "There's something in the house."

The hairs on the back of Oliver's neck bristled.

"Did she say *attacked*?" Anna asked.

One of the officers spoke into the radio then ran to the back of the house while the other comforted the dazed woman. The crowd had grown as word spread through the neighborhood. Eventually, additional officers arrived and surrounded the house.

The crowd stood helpless as two officers kicked in the front door. The sound of breaking glass came from the back side of the house as the police must have broken the window to unlock the door.

The ambulance arrived several nerve-racking minutes later, but by the time the paramedics loaded Madeline onto the gurney, the police had swept the entire house and emerged empty-handed. Whoever had attacked Madeline had somehow slipped away, leaving both doors locked from the inside.

CHAPTER NINETEEN

Two cracked ribs, a punctured lung, and a broken arm were small prices to pay for survival. Madeline spent several days in the hospital in the neighboring town. When the police swept the house, the bedroom looked as if it had been tilted on its side. The bed had been slammed against the wall, leaving large cracks in the plaster, and the entire contents of the room had been pushed to one side. It appeared that everything had nearly been sucked out of the window with Madeline. Although the police found no footprints, fingerprints, nor signs that an intruder had been inside, they did find the same small scratches on the door as those found at the other houses—several red scratches forming an obscure S shape.

Izzy tapped a knuckle on the hospital-room door.

"Come in," a voice said from around the corner.

Not only had Izzy insisted they visit Madeline in the hospital, but she'd nearly had a breakdown when Anna and Oliver brought back the news Madeline had been attacked. For someone who so adamantly voiced her dislike for Madeline, Izzy was oddly upset by the attack on the woman.

Madeline, usually primped and polished, lay exhausted in bed. Her hair was devoid of the extensions that gave it that extra bounce, and her face was ashen and wrinkled. When she saw Izzy, her gaze momentarily softened.

"We brought you some goodies," Izzy said, putting the wicker basket on the table. Madeline said nothing but seemed legitimately shocked to see the two of them.

"How are you feeling?" Oliver asked, trying to break the awkward silence.

Madeline looked at both of them, mouth open slightly.

"It's good to see you, Isabelle," she said, ignoring Oliver's question.

"Any news from the police?" Izzy asked, tears welling in her eyes.

"Not much. They didn't find anything in the house. If it wasn't for the catastrophe in the bedroom and those scratches on the door, they would probably think I was just a clumsy old biddy who took a tumble out the window," she replied.

"Did you see anything?" Izzy asked.

"Things are still a bit of a blur, but I heard a tapping noise. Over and over again. I was in the bedroom, ironing, and that's where it came for me. *Tap. Tap. Tap.* But the sound was everywhere, like it was inside my head. When it finally stopped, I turned to grab the phone and call Martin, and something hit me like a ton of bricks. I swear I saw a woman standing on the other side of the room. Couldn't see her face—it was covered by long black hair—but she was wearing a tattered nightdress. The police couldn't find her, though, and I'm beginning to think I imagined it. How could a woman have done so much damage?"

"That's terrible," Izzy said.

Madeline's comments put a knot in Oliver's stomach. "Do you remember anything else?" he asked, prying for additional info.

"No, just a *tap, tap, tap, like fingernails.* At first, I thought maybe Martin had forgotten his keys and was knocking on the door." She stared at her lap for a moment. "He's always losing his keys, the silly man. How's everything back at home? Complete chaos, I imagine."

"They've sent more officers from the neighboring district and the state patrol. The police have also implemented another curfew although I'm not sure what good that will do since two of the attacks occurred behind locked doors," Izzy replied.

Madeline looked down as if debating whether or not to say what was on her mind. She looked at Oliver. "For what it's worth... I'm sorry," she said.

"Sorry?" Oliver replied. The words had knocked him back a few steps.

"For giving you such a hard time—for having the Elders keep such a close eye on you. We should have listened to Eric. You had nothing to do with this, and that's clear to me now. I'm sorry that it took so long."

Oliver felt a twinge of anger. The Elders had made him feel like a prisoner. If he hadn't just learned the woman he saw in the field might have been responsible for the attack, he might have given Madeline a piece of his mind.

"Oh, I hadn't noticed," he lied. "Don't worry about it."

Who is this woman who comes bearing apologies? He didn't recognize Madeline nor Izzy, and the attack seemed to have broken down some invisible barrier between them.

"What the hell was that?" Oliver asked when he was safely out of Madeline's earshot.

"What are you talking about?"

"The tears, the apology. You hated that woman,

and I'm pretty sure she hated you too. Why so friendly now?"

"I don't hate her. Besides, she could use a little friendliness. We used to be good friends, actually."

"What? What happened between you two, then?"

"The town," Izzy replied. "I tried to get involved. Madeline encouraged me. But we clashed over everything. She's so traditional, and I wanted to liven things up a bit. I think the painting at the art show was the final straw, but things had been rough between us for some time. Oh, I feel terrible about how I've been to her. She could have died. This silly feud isn't worth it."

"Terrible?" Oliver replied. "She nearly put you out of business and has people spying on me."

Izzy shrugged. Oliver took a few deep breaths and tried to calm himself. Whatever feud had existed between Izzy and Madeline was the least of his problems. If the woman from the field was responsible for the attacks, he had come face-to-face with a murderer. *But why is she attacking the town, and will she come back for me?*

CHAPTER TWENTY

I zzy handed Oliver the bakery phone. "It's for you," she said.

He held up the receiver to his ear. "Hello?"

"Oliver, it's Eric. You got a minute?"

"Sure, what can I do for you?"

"I think we finally got our first big break, kid. One of Madeline's neighbors saw someone messing around with her front door on Halloween night. Think he's the one scratching those symbols in the wood with the tip of his cane."

Oliver's heart sank.

"What did he look like?"

"Funny you should ask. We probably never would have found the guy except he's wearing this god-awful blue suit. We brought the description over to the tavern yesterday, and the bartender recognized him right away. He's been staying in one of the rooms. We've been holding him at the station since last night."

"Well, that's great news. How can I help?" Oliver held out a tiny bit of hope that the man hadn't mentioned the coin, but why else would Eric be calling him?

"The guy says he stopped by the bakery the other day. He mentioned he spoke to you directly and asked about that coin you found at Francis's place."

"Uh, yeah, he did."

"And he said you referred him to us—told him we had it. Is that right?"

"Right," Oliver replied.

"And you and I both know you have the coin. So, why would you lie to him, and more importantly, why wouldn't you mention this somewhat bizarre interaction to me?"

"Um, I—"

"Either way, it doesn't matter now. We'll need the coin, though. Do you have it with you?"

"It's at home, but I can go grab it right now."

"I'll meet you at the house in fifteen. And I don't want to find out you've been keeping anything else from me. If this guy has anything to do with the murders, we could have questioned him a long time ago and maybe prevented the attack on Madeline."

"I'm sorry. It was a mistake, and it won't happen

again."

"Better not. See you soon."

Oliver hung up the phone and looked over at Izzy, who had been listening in on his side of the conversation. He felt guilty for keeping his encounter with the stranger from Eric.

"Someone's in trouble," Izzy said, leaning over the metal kitchen table. "What did you do?"

"I've got to go back to the house. They found the man who came in the other day and think he might have something to do with the attacks. Eric wants to stop by to pick up the coin. He was pissed because I didn't call and tell him when the guy came into the store that day."

He left the bakery and walked in the direction of Izzy's house. *What am I going to do?* The thought of handing the coin over to the police made Oliver sick to his stomach. He took solace in the fact that the mystery man was safely tucked away in police custody. *But where is the woman?*

He would have to turn the coin over to the police unless he ran, but that would make him look guilty. He had no way out of this, and soon he'd lose the coin and his only way to access Briarwood.

As he approached the house, Oliver noticed a large

lump of butterscotch fur on the front porch. Nekko eyed him as he walked across the grass. The front door had been left ajar.

He cautiously approached, picked up the plump tabby, and slowly pushed the door open. He put Nekko down on the living room floor, and she sauntered over to a patch of sunlight in front of the window.

The place was turned upside down. Books had been ripped off the shelves, Izzy's artwork had been toppled and torn, and the contents of the drawers and cubbies in the living room had been spilled onto the floor. Someone had come in search of the coin.

He heard a meek whimper from the other room. "Pan," he said under his breath. Oliver walked into the kitchen, peeking around the corner to ensure no one was waiting for him. The tiny corgi was nowhere in sight.

"Pan?" he whispered.

The whimper was coming from underneath the cart in the corner of the room. He knelt down and looked underneath. As soon as he made eye contact, Pan came scampering from under the cart and jumped at Oliver as if pleading to be saved.

"Oliver?" Eric shouted from the front door.

"Someone's broken in," he said. "The place is a mess—" A crash came from overhead. He wasn't sure what to do, so he froze, heart thumping louder than it ever had before.

The shouting must have tipped off the intruder. Oliver heard drawers being ripped from the dresser upstairs, followed by the sound of the entire dresser toppling to the floor. The intruder made their way down the hallway, seemingly overturning everything as they passed. Oliver edged toward the kitchen door, preparing to make a run for it.

"Stay there," Eric whispered, startling him. He'd peeked out from the living room doorway, gun drawn. "I'm going upstairs. If I say run, you run for the station. I've radioed for help." He disappeared into the living room.

"Police!" Eric shouted. "Come down slowly with your hands behind your head."

Oliver held his breath, as he often did when he was petrified. The chaos upstairs continued.

"We're coming up!" Eric shouted.

Who's we? Surely, he isn't going up by himself.

Oliver heard heavy footsteps on the staircase, and whoever was on a rampage upstairs seemed to have heard them too. The crashing stopped, and the hallway window shattered onto the roof of the back porch. Whoever was in the house was trying to escape out the second-floor window. Eric's boots boomed on the wooden floor as he ran toward the window before trudging back to the staircase.

Eric flew past Oliver and out the back door.

"Whoever it was is gone," Eric said, walking in from the back, several moments later. "Did you get a look at him?"

"Haven't moved," Oliver said, still frozen in fear. Eric crossed the kitchen and looked out the back window. "Dammit," he said under his breath.

Police cars arrived a few minutes later, as did a panic-stricken Izzy. While the police inspected the house, Eric sat with Oliver and Izzy at the kitchen table.

"Have you noticed anything missing?" Eric asked.

Oliver saw his opportunity. If the intruder had come looking for the coin, they clearly hadn't found it by the time Eric intervened. He could only hope it was still tucked away behind the baseboard.

"I came back for the coin. I left it on my bedroom dresser," he lied. "I haven't checked, but what if they came looking for it?"

Problem solved.

"We'll check it out."

Sure enough, no coin was to be found around Oliver's toppled dresser when he and Eric went searching for it.

Eric returned to the kitchen with a scowl.

"What's the matter?" Izzy asked.

"This puts us in a bit of a predicament. The man we have in custody clearly couldn't have broken in. The pattern here is somewhat similar—only no one was home at the time, thank God."

Oliver hated to think about what would have happened if someone had been home. *What if it had been Izzy?*

"So, we can assume whoever was responsible for this is also responsible for the other attacks. And that couldn't be our man in custody. The most we'll be able to charge him with is a few counts of destruction of property for carving signs into the doors."

"You and I both know it can't be a coincidence he happened to deface the three doors of three people who were viciously attacked. There's no way," Oliver said.

"Circumstantial," Eric replied. "It's just not enough. There's no evidence the guy was inside any of the houses, and clearly, he couldn't have broken into Izzy's while still in custody. We're going to have to let our friend go unless we find additional evidence that warrants a charge, and the odds aren't looking very good."

"What about the woman Madeline saw in the house the night of her attack?" Oliver asked.

"How do you know about that?" Eric replied.

"Madeline—she told us when we visited her in the hospital."

"She did say something about a woman, but we've found nothing to support it. We think she may have just been—"

"I saw her too," Oliver interrupted.

"Saw her? Where?" Eric asked.

"At the edge of the woods," he replied. "I went looking for the house, the one I told you about earlier. She confronted me—just stood and blocked my path back to Izzy's. My flashlight flickered, and by the time I got it working again, she was gone."

"What did she look like?"

"Skinny with long black hair and a dirty night-dress," Oliver replied. Once again, he left out the details about the secret town on the other side of the briars.

Eric gave Oliver a stern look. "All right then, looks like we've got some searching to do. We'll keep you posted if we find anything."

"What if she comes back?" Izzy asked. "We can't just stay here alone."

"If she—or whoever broke in—was looking for the coin, they've gotten what they came for. Perhaps our suspect has been telling the truth, and the person responsible did indeed steal the coin from him."

Oliver felt a twinge of guilt. If the intruder actually

was looking for the coin and found out Oliver still had it, they might come back. His lie would put Izzy in danger.

"Think you could keep someone out here tonight?" Oliver asked. "We might sleep a little better."

Eric nodded. "We'll post an officer outside for the night. We're going to have to let our suspect go this evening if we don't find anything strong enough to charge him. If you think of anything that might be helpful to us, give me a call. And if he bothers you again, let me know." He turned toward the door into the living room.

"Wait a sec," Oliver said. "You didn't get his name, did you? I asked him for it when he came to the bakery, but he didn't say."

"Hale," Eric replied.

"His name's Hale?" Oliver asked.

"At least, that's what he claims," Eric replied. "Simon Hale. Guy's got no identification on him, though, so all we have at this point is his word. Turns out the tavern still lets guests pay with cash."

"Isn't that at least a little suspicious?" Oliver asked.

"Suspicious, yes—illegal, no."

Eric wrapped up with the other officers in the living room and left to return to the station. Once the police finished sweeping the house, they packed up their gear and left, except for the officer who would be camping out in the front yard.

"Oliver, is it?" he asked, standing in the doorway.

"That's me," he replied.

"My name's Ben. They sent me over from Amberley. I'll be keeping an eye on the house tonight. If you need anything, just holler," he said, sticking out his hand for a handshake.

Izzy poked her head around the corner.

"And you must be Isabelle," Ben said.

Izzy came over to greet him, extending her arthritic hand as elegantly as it would allow.

"Call me Izzy, please," she said, batting her eyelashes.

Ben was well built and must have been several inches taller than Oliver, whose height already exceeded six feet. As he turned away from the door, Izzy looked over at Oliver and raised her eyebrows.

Oliver first had the thought after Simon visited the bakery that day. But the man spoke quite differently from those in Briarwood. The name confirmed it, though: Hale. Oliver *had* come face-to-face with Briarwood's *glorious leader*.

Once Ben returned to his cruiser and Izzy was busy cleaning up the living room, Oliver sneaked to the third floor. His room had been left in shambles. Clothes had been pulled from the dresser drawers and were strewn across the floor, and the toppled dresser had left a deep gash in the hardwood. He lifted the dresser out of the way and examined the wooden molding next to the bedroom door. The strip of wood sat perfectly in place, undisturbed by the intruder's rampage through the house. With a deep breath, he pulled the loose piece away, exposing the gold coin underneath.

CHAPTER TWENTY-ONE

Oliver had given up on sleep completely. He sat at the small desk in his room while Nekko lay on his pillow, enjoying her unexpected brush with luxury.

With Anna's help, he and Izzy had managed to clean most of the mess on the top two floors and sealed the broken window with cardboard and a few strips of duct tape.

The light from the desk lamp flashed across the coin in his hand as he examined the crow wrapped in tight vines. He mindlessly rubbed his thumb over the etchings, sympathizing with the dying bird. He too felt pulled into the briars and trapped in something he couldn't quite understand. Eric had released Simon that evening, finding no other evidence to link him to the murders, and Oliver hoped the man would buy the story of the stolen coin—hoped that Simon wasn't the one somehow responsible for the break-in. Somehow, Simon and the woman had to be linked. *But how?* He was sure he'd be able to find the answer in Briarwood.

A crash from the front yard broke his concentration. He ran toward the window to peer outside. The police cruiser was completely upended on the other side of the road, as if it had been picked up and thrown. The crash on the front lawn was followed by a bang at the front door. Panic set in, and he felt cold needles rise from his feet and up through his spine.

"Izzy!" he screamed, as if the sound of twisting metal and splintering wood hadn't been enough to wake her.

She slept on the second floor, and he slept on the third, so whoever had just broken in would get to Izzy first. Oliver ran down the stairs toward her room, coin clenched in his hand. As he reached the second floor, Izzy cracked her door.

"What's happening?" she asked in a quivering whisper.

"Lock the door and call the police," he replied. "Don't open it until they get here."

Oliver nearly tripped down the staircase to the first floor, heels sliding out from under him.

The front door had been ripped completely off the hinges, but he saw no one in the living room. He had nothing more to defend himself than his bare hands, but he crept around the corner into the kitchen— nothing there either. As he returned to the living room, he saw a silhouette in the front doorway. The same lanky figure he'd encountered in the field stood hunched, with jet-black hair hanging over her face. She raised a bony arm with open palm upturned, as if asking for something. He knew what she wanted, but he didn't budge.

She waited a moment and appeared to be displeased with his lack of response. She turned her head away from him and hobbled toward the staircase. *She's going for Izzy.*

"Looking for this?" he asked, holding the coin up between his thumb and index finger.

The woman's head snapped around, seemingly detached from the rest of her body. She smiled to reveal her jagged yellow teeth and held out her hand once more.

"You can't have it," he said. He had no idea where the sudden bravado came from.

She cocked her head, and he felt a sharp pain in his stomach, as if someone was grabbing him by his insides. The force pulled him upward. As his feet left the ground, he noticed everything else in the room was levitating too. The girl remained glued to the floor, but everything around her was floating.

Oliver tried to breathe, but his lungs refused to expand, either due to panic or the woman's telekinetic vice grip on his vital organs.

She's going to kill me.

As Oliver loosened his grip on the coin, a staccato pop came from the front door. The woman lurched forward and let out a bansheelike scream as she gripped her shoulder. Everything in the room—including Oliver—came crashing to the ground.

"Run!" Ben yelled from the doorway.

Oliver needed a moment to regain his bearings, however. As he stood, a curio cabinet whizzed by his head and crashed into the wall next to Ben. Oliver ran to the kitchen and managed to escape out the back door and slam it shut before the knives from the butcher block embedded themselves into its thick wooden frame.

How is she doing this?

He knew he wouldn't be able to outrun her for long, and he could hear the weeds shifting behind him. She was rapidly closing in, not running but gliding toward him. He turned his head to see the woman hovering across the field, her feet parting the tall weeds below. He had nowhere to go, nowhere that offered safety, except for possibly the briar patch. If the coin truly offered safe passage, crossing the briars might be his only hope.

When Oliver reached the patch, he leapt into the wall of thorns. As he did, the woman's bony hand wrapped around his ankle. Oliver had crossed the barrier, but she yanked his leg out from under him, and he fell flat on his face. He turned over as she slowly climbed his body. Her dark stringy hair hung on either side of his head, and she brought her face so close to his he could smell her acrid breath. Oliver traced her nose up to her eyes, but the shadow cast by the moonlight made it hard for him to see. At first, she appeared to have a sideways catlike pupil, but as his eyes adjusted, he realized that a line of stitches had sealed her right eye. Dried tears of blood crusted the skin under the sutures. The left eye stared at him with unblinking ferocity.

Oliver reached out to his side, searching for anything he might be able to use to defend himself. He ran his fingers over a large rock. With as much force as he could muster, he brought the rock crashing into the side of the woman's head. She let out a groan and fell limply onto the ground next to him. He scurried to his feet and ran toward the row of gaslights lighting the path to town, not daring to look back. *How was she able to follow me?* He hoped the blow to the head would incapacitate the woman—the creature—for a while, at least until he figured out what to do next.

"Over here, child!" someone called to Oliver from

the building next to him. A frail woman stood with broom in hand on the front porch of the building at the edge of the briars.

"Over here," she said again, beckoning him with the broom. Oliver had no time to consider the offer—it was either this or certain death—and ran toward her. She shuffled over to the front door and ushered him inside, latching the door behind them.

"Just sit down and stay silent," she whispered and blew out the oil lantern in the front window.

The room was completely dark, so Oliver sat where he was and leaned against a heavy wooden object. The woman perched underneath the window at the front of the store.

A few terrifying minutes passed as the two sat in complete silence. He heard a shriek in the distance, and it sounded as though the woman with the stitched eye was heading in the other direction.

"Who is she?" he whispered.

"The Witch," the woman replied.

"The Witch?" Oliver asked.

"The Briarwood Witch."

"Wha—" Oliver started but was interrupted by an abrupt pounding on the door. He felt gooseflesh form on his arms. Oliver held his breath as the two waited for the unwelcome visitor to leave.

Someone pounded again. "Constance, open the door!"

The woman struggled to get to her feet.

"No! Don't open it," Oliver whispered, but she had already unlatched the door. Three men, tall and rugged in stature, rushed into the building, nearly knocking Constance off her feet.

"Where is the stranger?" one of them asked.

"Who?" she replied.

The man held out his lantern to illuminate the interior of the building. Oliver attempted to shuffle behind the large wooden object, but they had already spotted him.

"Take him," the man said.

The two others rushed forward to grab Oliver by the legs and pull him into the center of the room. They lifted him to his feet and led him over to the door.

"Wait, the Witch," Oliver started.

"The Witch from whose curse we were free until you brought her back?" The man wrapped his leather glove around Oliver's throat. "We are well aware of the Witch."

As the band of men led Oliver from the building, the light from the lantern allowed him to see the inside. The place appeared to be a shop, filled with shiny metal baubles.

The men dragged Oliver past the town statue of

Nathaniel Hale and toward the town hall, just behind the square. They didn't ascend the large staircase to the main entrance but rather led him off to one side to a smaller wooden door. One of the men pounded on the door with his fist, and a small peephole slid open.

"Who is he?" the man behind the peephole asked.

"We found this trespasser running through town. He has brought the Witch back to torment us."

"And the glorious leader?" the man asked.

"No—no sign of the bastard."

"Praise be," the man replied.

The peephole slid closed, and Oliver heard a heavy *thunk* on the other side of the door as the man behind it slid a reinforcement bar out of the way.

Oliver was prodded inside the building. The door watchman returned to the short wooden stool next to the heavy wooden door. Once the men were inside, they barred the door and led Oliver down a narrow hallway. Decorative sconces lined the stone walls, hissing with the gas that fueled the flickering flames. The men opened the door to a tiny room, which was only dimly lit by the lamps in the hallway.

"You can't lock me up here," Oliver said. "She's chasing me. She'll kill all of us."

"No need to worry. We aren't going to lock you up here." The man pointed to a small wooden hatch in the center of the floor. "Your new home is down there."

The man unlatched the floor hatch and forced Oliver to descend the rickety wooden ladder into the darkness below. The hatch shut above him, and the men closed the door to the hallway, leaving Oliver in total darkness.

Oliver was in a complete panic. He tried to control his breath, but the black was closing in on him. He took slow careful steps in search of a wall to sit against. When he found the damp stone foundation, he slid to the ground. The floor below him was cold and wet, and he had already started to shiver.

Several minutes passed, and his breath slowly returned to normal. His senses sharpened in the darkness, and he could smell the dampness around him. As he sat in silence, he could swear he heard breathing on the other side of the room. A faint shuffling a few moments later confirmed something else was occupying the pit with him.

"Who's there?" Oliver's voice echoed against the seeping stone walls.

The shuffling stopped, but several moments passed before the stranger broke the silence. "Just a fellow unfortunate soul," he replied.

Oliver had heard the voice before.

"You were at the town hall meeting the other night, weren't you?" he asked. He recalled the man who'd stood in front of the crowd, waving his arms and trying to reestablish order.

"Indeed," the man replied. "Unfortunately, I was not able to restore my favor with the people of Briarwood. It's difficult to tell exactly how long I have been down here without the sunrise and sunsets to break up the days."

"Why are we down here? What's going on?" he asked.

"Ingratitude," the man replied. "Our glorious leader has been missing for some time now, and the town celebrates his absence. Simply disgraceful. He has protected us from the outside world, from those who'd seek to kill us. Without his protection, we will not be able to survive here."

"And who are you?"

"I am very fortunate to serve as our glorious leader's assistant. I tend to his daily business and ensure everything remains in order."

"And your name?" he asked.

"Oh." The man paused as if he couldn't remember. "Elias. And your name?"

"Oliver. I'd shake your hand if I could."

"Oliver... Oliver... an odd name. I don't recall seeing any Olivers on the town roster," Elias replied.

"I'm not from around here. I live on the other side of the briar patch."

The man was silent.

"Are you still there?" Oliver asked the darkness.

"Don't hurt me," Elias whispered, his voice trembling.

"Why would I—"

The door creaked in the room above him. The hatch flew open, and he was momentarily blinded by the flood of light as a lantern slowly descended into the pit.

"Boy! Come with me," someone yelled from above.

Oliver assumed he was "boy," approached the ladder, and began to climb. The guard grabbed him by an arm and pulled him up the rest of the way. This guard was probably the size of the last three men combined. He bound Oliver's hands with rope and led him upstairs to the meeting hall. The room was just as he remembered from the other night, alive and full of furious people—only this time, they focused their anger on him. The guard led him through the main entrance and dragged him down the carpeted aisle leading to the front of the room. The barrage of screams and insults from the crowd was overwhelming. *What are they going to do to me?*

The guard forced him into a chair facing the crowd.

A man emerged from one of the rows of benches and walked toward him before turning to address the audience. "Quiet!" he shouted, trying to bring order to the crowd.

He yelled several more times, and silence slowly crept over the mob.

"Thanks to all for being here," he said. "As we are all aware, the Witch was spotted on the outskirts of town in the presence of this outsider."

"Kill the outsider!" a woman shouted from one of the benches.

Oliver felt ill.

"Now, patience, please!" the man said. "Before we determine punishment, we must first understand the dark forces this boy used to bring her back. Perhaps we can banish her once more." He turned to Oliver. "Well, boy, explain yourself."

"She was chasing me," he sputtered. "She attacked my home, and I ran. She chased me through the briar patch."

The crowd collectively gasped, and any remaining chatter stopped abruptly.

"That's absurd. No one but the Witch and our glorious leader passes through the briar patch."

"It's true. It's true. I can show you how." Oliver fumbled in his pocket and pulled out the gold coin.

The man nodded to one of the guards, who approached Oliver and took it from him. As soon as he saw the etching on the front, he dropped it on the ground and took a step backward.

"It's the Briarwood Key," the guard said, as if terrified by the dull coin on the floor. The crowd broke into shouts and commotion.

"Where did you find this?" the interrogator asked.

Oliver immediately regretted his decision to reveal the coin.

"Where?" the man shouted. He gripped one end of the table in front of Oliver and flipped it over and out of the way.

"I just found it," he stammered.

"Found it where?"

"In-in a flower bed back home."

"Why did you bring the Witch back here?"

"I told you—she was chasing me. I didn't mean to. I'm sorry," Oliver said, panicked tears streaming down his face.

"So she came for you?"

"I think she wants the coin back," he replied.

"And she thinks you possess it?"

Oliver nodded.

"Very well then," the man said, relaxing his stance. Oliver exhaled, taking a premature sigh of relief. The man clenched his fist and took a quick jab at Oliver's face. The chair tilted over, and Oliver smacked the back of his head on the floor. Everything went dark.

CHAPTER TWENTY-TWO

S evere pain brought Oliver back to the waking world. His head pounded as if a pickaxe were pecking away at the inside of his skull. He tried to move his arms, but his hands had been bound behind him, held together by a frayed length of old rope that scratched and burned his wrists as he struggled. The setting was familiar, and he recognized the uneven grid of stones surrounding him. He had been propped up in the middle of the town square. The statue of Nathaniel Hale lay in ruins next to him, deformed by its toppling. He stood on the statue's pedestal, tied to some sort of wooden beam mounted against its base.

Oliver looked over at the broken statue of the town's founder. He thought of Elias, the regal keeper of order, who was locked away in a dank pit, hidden from the rest of the world. *This is a coup.* The glorious leader —Simon, Oliver was almost sure—had disappeared, and the townspeople had clearly taken the opportunity to wrestle power from what little rule remained.

But why am I here?

The square was vacant, and the lights from the surrounding buildings had been extinguished, even those in the town hall. He had no concept of the time but guessed it was early morning. The only sources of light were the gas streetlights bordering the square. The silence was overwhelming, and Oliver would rather have been in the presence of an angry mob than in isolation, wondering what fate awaited him. He wanted to go home, back to Izzy, Anna, Nekko, and Pan—to a time before his discovery of the coin. *And what of them? Are they safe? Has Simon come for them too?* He was trapped, both confined to the stone pedestal and confined to this strange world beyond the briars. Oliver no longer possessed the coin that allowed him to cross over, and he might very well never leave the place again.

Something caught his eye as one of the streetlights flickered in his periphery. An odd stream of fog slowly rolled in and consumed the lantern, suffocating the light in its opaque mist. It flowed inward from the corner of the square, extinguishing the street lamps, one by one, along with any hope that Oliver would walk away from Briarwood alive.

The Witch is here.

The sickening realization washed over him. *She thinks you have the coin?* This question had been the last posed to Oliver before the man in the town hall sent him crashing to the floor. *She wants me.* Oliver was the sacrificial lamb, and perhaps the Witch would leave the town alone once she had him.

The mist consumed an entire corner of the square, like water creeping over the bow of a sinking ship. He struggled to free himself from his bonds and rubbed his wrists raw against the splintering rope. A slender silhouette hobbled from the mist. For a moment, Oliver held out hope it was someone—anyone—other than the Witch, but her pigeon-toed creep and stringy black hair were unmistakable. She moved awkwardly, lanky limbs clumsily stepping toward the center of the square, as if her legs had been broken multiple times and improperly healed. She tilted her head, causing her hair to slink to one side.

Oliver felt a pair of hands on his as someone gripped the ropes behind him.

"Hold still and say nothing," the person whispered from behind.

He could feel the vibration of a knife against the rope. As the binding fell away, the mysterious savior grabbed his wrists, holding them together and preventing him from pulling free.

"When I tell you to flee, turn round and run as fast as your legs can carry you. Not until I say."

"Got it," he replied.

The woman behind him whistled, and a flaming object flew toward the Witch. The vessel exploded against the stone, sending bright-orange flames spilling out onto the ground. The light from the flame illuminated the Witch, and Oliver noticed the dried blood on the side of her head from where he'd struck her and the patch of crimson on her shoulder from Ben's bullet.

"Run!"

He turned and hopped down from the tall stone, his feet landing awkwardly on the uneven bricks below. He stumbled forward and regained his footing, running in the direction of the woman in front of him. Her long brown hair whipped in the wind, strands blowing chaotically in the breeze. She sprinted toward one of the storefronts.

A loud screech came from behind, and Oliver turned to see the Witch's feet rise from the ground and hover over the flame.

As they approached the storefront, the door swung open, and a man on the other side waved them in. He crossed the threshold as the man held up a bottle resembling a Molotov cocktail, at least the ones Oliver had seen in movies. He lit the rag, which hung loose from its neck, with a candle and flung it at the Witch, who was now halfway across the square. The makeshift bomb exploded below her feet, and flaming accelerant splattered into the air, scorching the bottom of her dress. She let out another howl just as the door shut in Oliver's face.

"That'll slow her but not for long. Lift the hatch," the woman said.

The small candle provided just enough uneven light for Oliver to make out the broad shoulders of the man who had opened the door. He shuffled over to the center of the room and pulled the floor rug back, revealing a wooden hatch beneath it. Oliver had flashbacks of the dungeon and the terrifying darkness that came with it, but if these people had planned to lock him away, they wouldn't have bothered to save him. The man's lumbering form disappeared into the hatch below.

"Hurry," the woman said, pushing him from behind. He climbed down the shallow staircase, and she followed, pulling the rug back over the door before shutting it behind her.

The room was completely silent except for the few shallow breaths escaping from Oliver's hand-cupped mouth. A sudden pulse of pressure caused the hatch to creak above them. The front door of the store splintered and cracked as it was ripped away from its hinges and sent flying across the room. Breaking glass and debris rained down on the floor above them, sounding like an unexpected hailstorm. Oliver could visualize the emaciated Witch floating over the floor above them, bare feet pointing downward like a ghostly ballerina in midjump. No one said a word but merely sat in silence, and Oliver weighed whether or not it would have been better to have been ripped apart in the town square than to die in a deep, damp hole.

After several tense moments, the back door slammed open. Perhaps the Witch assumed they had escaped out the back.

"Light the lantern."

Oliver couldn't tell who the woman was speaking to, but a moment later, he heard a noise that sounded as though someone was scraping two rocks together, accompanied by several sparks. After a few strikes from the flint, the wick of the metal lantern caught fire and cast a warm glow over the small earthen room and its inhabitants. Now that Oliver had a clear look at her face, he recognized the woman who had saved him. She was the one who'd called Elias a 'weasel' in the town meeting. *But why did she save me?* The question still lingered. Several wooden barrels lined the walls, some filled to the brim with a variety of root vegetables and others capped off with wooden lids, obscuring their contents.

"How long should we wait here?" Oliver asked.

The man shuffled to the other side of the room and slid one of the wooden barrels out of the way, revealing a small tunnel, carved out of the dirt wall behind it.

"The tunnel will take us next door," the woman said. Oliver had no clue who these people were, but they'd already saved him from certain death, and the tunnel was a much better alternative than facing the Witch, who had ravaged the storefront above them. The tunnel itself was just large enough to squeeze his body through, and he had to army crawl his way to the other side. The walls had been reinforced with a basic wooden frame, but his mild claustrophobia made them feel as if they were collapsing in on him, slowly surrounding him in a mud tomb. When he made it to the other side, he was relieved to find a formal basement, much like the one underneath Izzy's bakery. The stone floor was cool against the palms of his hands as he pushed himself up onto his feet.

The trio gathered around a large wooden table placed in the middle of the room. For a moment, Oliver sat there, facing the two complete strangers who had just risked their lives to save his.

Perhaps due to the throbbing pain in the back of

his head or the trauma of what had just happened, the only thing he could think to ask was, "Who are you?"

The woman shot a look at the man across the table.

"I'm Mercy," she said, leaning over the table to shake his hand. She must have been in her early thirties, but her hand was coarse and calloused, as though it had seen decades of physical labor. "And he's my brother, Gideon," she said, nodding her head toward the beefy fellow across the table.

He appeared to be the same age but was three or four times her size. He said nothing but replied with a simple smile and nod.

"Don't expect much of a conversation with him. Took a blow to the throat a few years back. His voice never recovered."

Gideon nodded in affirmation.

"And your name?" Mercy asked.

"I'm Oliver."

"It's a pleasure to meet you, Oliver," Mercy said.

"Why did you save me?" he asked.

"Didn't have much of a choice now, did we?" she replied. "You are the only one, aside from Hale and the Witch, who has ever crossed the briars—the only outsider to enter the town since I've been alive. Thought maybe you could show us a way out."

"Simon Hale? Why do you call him Hale when everyone else calls him 'the glorious leader'?"

"It's mostly for show. Most in this town hate the man, but he'll sic the Witch on you if he gets wind of disobedience. Hale runs this town—has for the last few decades. Comes from a long line of great leaders although that trait seems to have skipped right over him."

"A line started by Nathaniel Hale," Oliver filled in.

"Correct. The family has passed down control of the town for generations, but Hale is the last in the line, aside from his daughter, but she could hardly pass as human."

"His daughter?"

"The very same witch who's been giving you hell," she replied. "She's Simon's daughter. There are whispers the man is magically impotent. With the family name comes family magic. It flows down the bloodline but must have skipped a generation with Simon. Hale struggled to keep control of the town until the birth of his daughter. The Witch has more power than all of the Hale ancestors combined, but something isn't right with her—not enough air to the brain during childbirth. Still, she can bend the world around her—control things with her mind."

Oliver could still feel the odd sensation of being lifted by his insides. "All the Hales could do this? Except for Simon?"

"Not exactly. Magic shows itself differently for

everyone. Thomas Hale could cause others to see things—unimaginable horrors."

Oliver's mind was still struggling to follow. "So, this magic—is it just the Hales, then? What about you? Can you do it too?"

Gideon put his hand to his mouth but couldn't keep the snicker from escaping through his fingers.

"Heavens no!" Mercy laughed. "There have been rumors of others like the Hale family, but those children rumored to show similar traits tend to go missing. Simon doesn't like to be challenged."

"What about Simon's wife? What happened to her?"

"She died in childbirth. He could have saved her, but he insisted on saving the children instead."

"Children?"

"The Witch was a twin, actually. They managed to save her although 'saved' is a relative term, but the boy only lived for a few years. Simon chains her like a beast during the day and sets her loose on the townspeople at night—anyone who dares to disobey him. Only one or two have come into contact with her and lived to tell the tale, but most simply vanish."

"I still can't get her eyes out of my mind. One of them is—"

"Stitched shut." Mercy looked up from the table, face solemn. "I remember them too."

"You saw?"

"A long time ago. I'll never forget that wretched tapping sound. The three of us were working late in the shop one night."

"Three of you?"

"My husband, Ezekiel, Gideon, and me. We all pay a protection fee, a kind of tax Elias collects throughout the year. Business was slow, and we couldn't pay the increased fee. Didn't go over well with Simon. It's the scratches in the door. That's how the Witch knows. He scratches a pattern in with the tip of his cane, like a curse, and that somehow draws her. Once he's marked your door, you are destined for death. We heard the tapping at the door. Must be her fingernails, tracing the pattern. But then we heard the tapping everywhere. We knew for certain the Witch was coming for us, but there was no place for us to run, no place to hide but this very basement."

"He charges a fee to protect you from his own daughter?" he asked.

"The fee pays for our protection from those outside the briars—protection from you, actually. According to Hale, we're under constant threat from those outside the woods. That was one reason why you received such a harsh welcome. He claims there is an evil force trying to break into the town—trying to kill us all. But some in the town have grown skeptical. The only threat seems to be from Simon himself and his wretched daughter."

"So he set her loose on you," Oliver prodded for her to continue the story.

"When she came bursting through the door, she sent Gideon flying like a rag doll. The last thing he would ever say was 'Run!' He hit his neck on the wooden table. Ezekiel made me hide in the basement. I can still remember his face, pressed against the crack in the door, just before he pushed it shut. I knew I would never see him alive again, and I was right. Everything important was to be stripped away. His scream—it still haunts my dreams. I'm not sure exactly what happened next, but I could hear him being dragged across the floor, the heels of his boots catching the edges of the floorboards. So, like a fool, I opened the door. I just couldn't sit there and wait, so I cracked the door to peek out into the store. When I saw his face, I nearly fainted. His jaw looked as if she had tried to tear it off. Just before she vanished into the night, she whipped her head round, as if she knew I was watching. That's when I saw her eyes, one stitched shut and the black of the other runny like a broken egg yolk. I don't know why she spared us—maybe she had gotten what she came for—but I swear she saw me. Eventually, she turned round and faded into the night."

Mercy stopped. Although she was sitting with two

others in the basement, she appeared to be alone, isolated by anguish. She was a million miles away, thoughtlessly stroking her long brown locks. Somehow, her features had softened in that moment, revealing a vulnerability hidden behind a mask of austerity. Oliver wasn't sure what to say, so he said nothing but just sat with them in the impromptu moment of silence.

Gideon reached across the table and put a hand on hers. This seemed to lull her out of the temporary daydream.

"Sorry," she said. "Somehow we managed to keep the shop going—I don't know how. But something started to happen after that. I began to notice subtle gestures, mumblings of discontent when people would visit. There were others who wanted to break free from Simon's oppression—those who had lost loved ones because of him. So I began to pry, very cautiously. A few groups of people exist in this town, those who want to bring their *glorious leader* back, who fear what will happen without his protection, and those who rejoiced when he stepped through the briars a few weeks ago and never returned."

"Which side has the coin, then? The coin is the only thing keeping him out of Briarwood," Oliver said.

Mercy looked down at the table. "Not either side, unfortunately. The man who nearly broke your nose... he's Richard Bennett. He sits on a third side, those who recognize the tremendous opportunity that presents itself when a tyrant leaves an empty throne behind."

"He wants the power for himself?" Oliver asked.

"And he'll be testing the key in short order."

"But why leave if he's vying for power?"

"The power to leave is the greatest power one can have in this town, aside from control of the Witch. It brings true freedom and access to all the knowledge of the outside world," she replied. "Simon brings artifacts back whenever he crosses over. Sometimes it's new technology, seeds, medicine, and other things we need to live. If Bennett is able to cross over—if he has the key-it's only a matter of time before others rally behind him."

"Then we have to get it back," he said.

"Absolutely right," she replied. "Fortunately, we have a few eyes and ears around town who will let us know when he wanders to the woods. He'll use the Witch as an excuse to take control, promising to keep the townspeople safe. If he's smart, he'll find Simon when he's on the other side and do away with him. If rumor is true, Simon is useless without his witch, and they are currently separated by the briars."

"And what are we going to do when Richard goes to the woods?" he asked.

Oliver had forgotten Gideon was in the room with them, his silence causing him to disappear against the stone backdrop of the cellar. But at this question, Gideon hopped up and walked across the room. A heavy canvas sack of flour dangled from an old rope anchored to a ceiling beam. With one heavy swing, he brought his fist crashing into the flour sack, snapping the rope and sending the makeshift punching bag flying. It burst on the hard floor, flour spewing into the air like dust escaping from a beaten rug.

"I may settle for a sword myself, but I believe Gideon has captured the general spirit of what we intend to do. If we don't take the coin now, we may never have another chance."

CHAPTER TWENTY-THREE

Word came of Bennett's planned march to the edge of the woods as the sun slowly crept over the horizon. A young boy tapped on the front door of the shop, and Mercy brought the news to Oliver and Gideon in the cellar.

"It's time," she said. "We must go back through the tunnel."

Oliver held his breath as he moved through the narrow space as quickly as he could. He had no idea how Gideon managed to squeeze through since the walls nearly touched his shoulders on either side, but somehow, he managed.

After the journey through the tunnel, Gideon attempted to lift the wooden hatch. He strained against it, but something must have fallen on top of it. He took his fist and pounded it against the planks.

Oliver heard the cautious creak of floorboards above his head.

"Mercy?" someone asked through the slats.

"We can't lift the door," she replied.

"Oh, praise be! I was worried sick," the person responded. "The cabinet's toppled over, and I can't lift it. Come round front."

After another claustrophobic trip through the tunnel, Oliver climbed the basement stairs to enter the storefront above them. He had been curious to discover the business in which Mercy and Gideon dealt and was somewhat surprised to find the walls of the store were lined with clothing.

"We must go next door. I'll check to make sure no one watches. Gideon, find Oliver something to wear," Mercy said, stepping outside.

Gideon tapped Oliver on the shoulder and held out a set of clothes. Certainly, the townsfolk would recognize him in his normal garb, which was horribly out of place amidst the town's odd fashion. He took the pair of brown cotton trousers, the olive-green button up, and the overcoat draped across Gideon's massive forearm and changed in the corner of the store. Gideon had also set aside a pair of dark leather boots, which would surely hold up better in the woods than Oliver's old sneakers. As he finished buttoning his shirt, a black derby caught his eye, hanging on the wall next to him. He wouldn't have been able to pull off the hat back home, but this wasn't home.

"What about that?" he asked, pointing at it. "Need something to cover up my face, right?"

Gideon shrugged, and Oliver grabbed the hat from the wall.

After a few moments, Mercy returned and beckoned them to follow. They quickly shuffled outside and to the building next door. Oliver caught a brief glimpse of the sunrise, which cast a peaceful glow on the square. It probably wouldn't be long until it was speckled with townsfolk going about their daily errands. He wondered if they lived their lives like the people in Christchurch, deadly witch and murderous leader aside. He read the wooden sign above the storefront, one he had been too in a hurry to notice before. A painted pocket watch adorned the front, and its chain underlined the sign's text, which simply said Clockmaker. Oliver could only imagine the damage the Witch had caused amidst such a delicate operation.

Mercy knocked on the wooden frame that had once held a door. A vibrant-red sheet hung in place of the heavy oak. The fabric was a flimsy replacement, and she brushed it aside to enter the store. The door itself still lay on the other side of the room, broken into splintered pieces scattered in a sea of glass and intricate watch mechanisms. Oliver felt a slight pang of guilt, knowing all this damage had been caused in an attempt to save him.

He hadn't been able to see the contents in the darkness, but now the sunlight from the window illuminated them, bouncing off glass faces and polished metal. The room was lined with ticking clocks. Wall clocks of various shapes and sizes hung on the patterned wallpaper, and several taller grandfather clocks sat on the floor, causing flashbacks to Oliver's office cube and Mr. Sally's angry spittle shower. His days in the city seemed so far away now. These clocks were different, though. The bodies were sculpted metal, and the intricate inner workings, typically hidden behind a box of carved wood, were on display for the world to see. The grandfather clocks had moving gears running down the lengths of their bodies. He knelt to get a closer look. As the gears rotated and shifted in the clock's body, they created the illusion of a pendulum swaying back and forth. But the pendulum was just that, a mechanical illusion.

The Clockmaker stood in the center of the room, sweeping his professional life into a heap on the wooden floor. His wispy gray hair billowed from the sides of his head like puffs of cotton candy although the top of his head was slick and barren.

"I'm so sorry, Father," Mercy said.

At first, he didn't respond but simply stared into the pile.

"Just things," he said, after a long pause. "Things are replaceable... daughters are not." He looked up at her with tired eyes magnified by a round set of wire-framed spectacles and underlined in bags undoubtedly caused by his daughter's well-intentioned rebellion. The man had a slight hunch, perhaps caused by hours of tinkering with tiny gears and cogs. His apron hung loose from his body, somewhat masking his frame behind a curtain of forest green.

"Bennett is going to the briars. We came for weapons," she said.

The Clockmaker let out a sigh and gestured toward the back room. The walls were lined with shelves of tools and containers of tiny pieces and screws. Half a dozen wooden barrels sat inconspicuously in the corner. Gideon wrapped his thick fingers around the cap of one of the barrels and jostled it loose. The old oak container had been filled to the brim with rice. His hand disappeared, up to the elbow, into the sand-like grains. He fished around for a moment, and the shuffling rice sounded like a warm spring shower. Then he pulled his hand out, gripping the handle of a long metal broadsword. After another search of the barrel, Gideon's hand emerged again, holding a leather wrap.

"I have a gift for you too," the Clockmaker said from the other room. When they returned to the front of the store, he was fiddling with the side of a mahogany display case. With a slight tug, he pulled off the dark wooden back panel, revealing a compartment hidden behind the cabinet's false back. The light caught the bottom of a purple velvet bag, which he carefully removed from the secret cubby. They followed him to the counter as he removed the object from the bag. At first, the weapon appeared to be just another blade, about a forearm's length, with the same detailed designs and carvings as the clocks adorning the walls. Upon closer inspection, Oliver noticed the flourishes on the blade guard were actually gun hammers, and the decorative metal rounds, which extended along the sword like pipes from an organ, were barrels. The handle was curved, not quite as much as a handgun, but still enough to allow for comfortable aim at a target.

"How long did this take?" Mercy asked, mesmerized by the beautiful filigree etched in the metal.

"Nearly a year," he replied.

"After the attack?" Mercy asked.

"I started after the attack, but with Simon gone, I knew it was only a matter of time before you came for the weapons. I am dreadfully behind on clock repairs, but I managed to finish this a few weeks ago." He pulled another item from the velvet bag, a brown leather belt, which held a line of bullets in perfectly sized loops.

"Do be careful," he said, sliding the belt across the counter. "And promise you will come back alive."

Mercy placed her hand on her father's. "I promise," she said. "But if we don't go now, we may lose our chance."

"Then be on your way," he replied.

"We'll send the others for the rest of the weapons when it's time," she said.

"How many others?" Oliver asked.

"Depends on how many keep their word—maybe ten or more." Mercy unwrapped the two sheathed daggers Gideon had pulled from the rice barrel. "Something to protect yourself," she said, handing them to Oliver.

And what exactly am I supposed to do with these? Oliver gripped the sculpted metal handles and tried to imagine himself fighting off a pack of angry townspeople, or worse, the Witch herself. His engineering degree hadn't trained him in the skills of war—he must have slept through that lecture.

Mercy slid a bullet into each of the barrels and wrapped the belt around her waist. "Shall we?" she asked, tucking the blade into the customized holster built into the side of the belt.

Although Gideon's sword was nearly as long as his leg, he concealed it beneath his crimson trench coat.

CHAPTER TWENTY-FOUR

Oliver guided Mercy and Gideon to the edge of the briar patch, where he had crossed over from Christchurch. The tangle of trees cast an ominous shadow on the unlikely trio as they looked out across the field. The scene was made of the same earth, with the same features as before, but he saw no evidence of humanity on the other side. Izzy's house on the hill was gone, as were all the hives and other artifacts of her existence. His heart dropped at the thought of never being able to see Izzy again.

He patted his empty pocket, where the Briarwood coin had once been. *It must work both ways.* The coin made it possible to see Briarwood from the outside, and the magic surrounding it must have also sheltered the people of Briarwood from seeing Christchurch.

Although he couldn't see the house, he did notice

the stark difference in the tree line on the other side of the patch. The deep greens of the Briarwood forest collided with the autumn leaves of Christchurch, almost as if an invisible forcefield was shooting up through the center of the patch and separating the two worlds and seasons within them.

Gideon picked up a long, curved stick and stuck it firmly into the briars. The vines wrapped around it, pulling it free from his hands. This caught him by surprise, and he nearly crushed Oliver's foot when he stepped backward from the patch.

"Let us wait over there." Mercy pointed at a downed tree that must have been at least three feet in diameter. The gap between the trunk and the earth had been covered on one side with branches and falling leaves. They wedged themselves up against it—a perfect hiding spot from the view of anyone approaching.

Oliver had nearly nodded off when the crunch of footsteps on the forest floor awoke him. Branches snapped, and leaves crackled under several sets of heavy boots. He pressed himself closer to the tree trunk as the pack of men marched past.

"Here," one of them said, walking toward the edge of the patch.

Oliver peered through a small crack in the trunk. He could count five men and held out five fingers behind him for the others to see. He panicked at the thought of having to confront them.

Five men? How can the three of us take five men? Panic set in. *What am I doing here? Why did I agree to this?* He wasn't a fighter, yet he was facing possible injury and death.

He immediately recognized the man who had left an enormous welt on his forehead. Bennett led the pack, and all were heavily armed with makeshift weapons. He reached into a small coat pocket and pulled out a shiny metal object, which he held up for the others to see.

"The two of us shall go through," Bennett said, patting the man next to him on the shoulder, "and the rest will stand guard and wait for our return."

The men nodded in agreement.

Bennett took a step toward the patch, and the vines shifted as if cast away by the invisible aura surrounding the coin. As he reached the edge, he let out a grunt and stopped suddenly. He seemed to struggle, his torso twisting as he tried to pull himself free from the ground, which somehow gripped his shoes like some sort of muddy cement.

Oliver tapped the two others and motioned for them to stick their heads out over the fallen tree.

Bennett fought the force for several seconds before a rustling from the trees above him caught the attention of the trio hiding behind the tree trunk. A swirl of deep-black hair descended from the trees, its fall somehow slowed like a fluttering leaf in the wind. The band of men saw the Witch but could do little more than stand and stare except for one who turned tail and ran toward the town. She fell onto all fours behind Bennett, who was still frozen in place. As she rose, her limbs contorted and cracked as if her body wasn't properly built to stand. At full height, she was but half of Bennett's, but she compensated by hovering above the ground until she faced the back of his head.

Oliver had never heard the brittle crack of human bone before, but the sound would be difficult to forget. The upper half of Bennett's torso twisted round, while his feet stayed firmly in place. He was face-to-face with the Witch, who stood unflinching as Bennett let out a bloody scream. Oliver wanted to run—needed to run— but surely that would call her attention to him. *But couldn't she have seen us from the trees?*

Perhaps his muscles were tensing from the sudden trauma, or perhaps due to pure resolve, Bennett somehow still clutched the coin. Blood had started to soak his shirt at the waist, and his pants were quickly changing color as they turned a deep crimson. The Witch turned her head slightly, looking at the coin clasped in his hand. As she twisted her head, so twisted Bennett's wrist, resulting in several sharp popping sounds. The man must have been in shock because he let out no cries of pain. He released his grip on the coin, and as soon as he did, the invisible force seemed to release its grip upon him. He fell backward—or forward, depending on perspective—into the briars. The vines curled around him, ensnaring his limbs and drawing blood from the cuts caused by the sharp thorns. Without the key, he would surely be consumed.

The Witch bent over to pick up the coin—the object she had been hunting for some time—but as she did, a wooden hammer swung down and struck her in the side, sending her stumbling into a tree. When she had released Bennett from her grip, the other men snapped out of their momentary panic. They approached the fallen Witch as the grizzled black-smith-looking fellow who had struck her stood over the coin. Gideon started to rise from behind the trunk, but Oliver placed a hand on his shoulder and pulled him back down behind the tree. The man picked the coin up from the forest floor. When he turned to face his cohort, his body shuddered, and he fell backward, stiff as a board. One of the band's makeshift swords protruded from his chest, and the man from whom the Witch had stolen it stood clutching his throat, trying to keep the spewing blood inside his body.

The remaining slipshod soldier hung in the air. The Witch turned to face him, and Oliver saw his opportunity. He couldn't let her cross into Christchurch or reunite with Hale. Simon was powerless without her, and she seemed to harm only those who stood between her and the coin. Without Simon pulling the strings, she had no mission but to track it down. If Oliver could just make it back across the briars, she would have no one to chase, and he could ensure Simon caused no additional harm to Christchurch.

"We can't let her take it. Stay here. I'll try to come back if I can," he whispered to his two companions.

Mercy grabbed his shoulder as he began to rise. "She will kill you."

"I can make it. It's either this or we all die. We can't beat her like this. Go back to Briarwood. She has no reason to chase you without the coin."

Mercy pulled her ammo belt free from her waist and handed it to Oliver. "Take this, then, and be careful."

He set his daggers on the ground and tightened the belt around his waist before quietly climbing over the tree and toward the body of the impaled man. He twisted the coin loose from the man's sausage fingers and edged toward the patch. The Witch had been momentarily distracted by the man hanging in the air. She seemed to be playing with him, like a cat playing with a rodent. The man began to scream as Oliver reached the edge of the briars, and he turned to see the poor soldier's mouth open inhumanly wide. He thought back to the Christchurch victims, turned back toward the patch, and broke into a full sprint.

The roses had begun to bloom once again, seemingly fueled by the body of the contorted revolutionary who had fallen into them. Oliver had made it halfway across when a scream came hurtling toward him. The Witch had sent the last soldier flying into the patch, but he collided with something midflight, and his yells suddenly ceased.

Oliver didn't stop to look—couldn't stop if he wanted to survive—until he made it out the other side of the briars. As he passed over the last group of brambles, he slid to a halt and turned to face the other direction. The last soldier had fallen somewhere in the middle of the patch, and the Witch was standing on the other side, separated from the key and powerless to harm him. She lingered there for a moment, frame hunched with her arms at her sides. Then, as if filled with a sudden burst of rage, she thrust her arms forward, her lips releasing an echoing wail. He could almost see her anger in the air, but the scream stopped at the barrier and reverberated with such force that it knocked her backward, her head like a comet trailed by a stream of tangled hair. The air above the briars seemed to sparkle, outlining the shape of a bubblelike curve extending from the center of the patch.

Oliver turned to face the house on the hill and was greeted by the familiar sunny-sided building. A minute before, the landscape on this side of the briars was barren, free from any signs of human intervention.

He trudged forward as the raindrops started to fall, but he didn't care—he was almost home. As he crossed the field, his eyes watered. For a few moments, when he was tied to the post in the Briarwood square, he thought he would never return to Christchurch and would never see Izzy and Anna again. He felt the same fear in the pit of his stomach when he looked upon the vacant hill, where Izzy's house had once stood.

Although the sky had darkened, the house lights were off, and Oliver noticed no signs of life from the outside. Even the bees seemed to be slowing down for the season. *Maybe she's at the police station.* He hoped the police had found a reason to keep Simon in custody.

A line of yellow police tape crossed the back of the door, and a note, forbidding entry, hung in the window.

What the hell is going on?

Surely, they wouldn't have kicked Izzy out of her own house to investigate the attack.

Oliver walked around to the front of the house. The same sign hung in the front window. The upended police cruiser had been towed away, leaving deep scars in the ground where it had landed.

The only other thing he could think to do was to walk across town to the police station.

As he rounded the bend by the market, Oliver decided against the station in favor of Anna's cottage. Two police cruisers sat across the street, keeping an eye on the market goers. He received several glares as he walked by and must have looked insane in his drenched overcoat and obscure wardrobe. Even if he hadn't looked as though he'd lost his mind, he certainly felt that way. He'd just seen several people murdered before his eyes and had left those who had saved him behind with the murderer. The Witch had no reason to hurt them though, since they didn't possess the coin—at least he hoped. Still, the guilt remained. The events of the past few hours swirled around in his head, but he didn't have time to be overwhelmed by them. He had to ensure that Izzy was safe and Simon was safely locked away. He stuffed his emotions into the back of his brain to deal with later.

Anna's cottage was seemingly immune to the chaos around it. He tapped his knuckle on the door and heard movement inside. He felt a wave of relief when Anna's face appeared through the crack in the door. When she saw him, she threw the door open and wrapped her arms around him.

"Thank God!" she said, tears starting to flow.

"Where's Izzy?" he asked.

"They don't know. We thought something terrible happened to you. We can't find her." She pulled him inside, and a flurry of scampering paws and corgi fur greeted him as Pan ran to his feet and leapt against his legs.

"Hey, bud," he said, bending down to address the neglected pup.

The sight of Pan was too much for him, and he completely lost it, tears dripping onto the dog's soft fur. Nekko lounged on the back of Anna's sofa, still a symbol of feline aloofness.

"Where have you been?" Anna asked.

"The Witch chased me to the woods, and—"

"Witch? What are you talking about?" she asked.

"The Witch," he said, wiping his eyes. "The woman who's been attacking everyone. She came for us. That officer, Ben I think, saw it all. He was the only reason I was able to get away."

"Ben?" she asked. "Oliver, he was killed. They found him inside the house. Somebody cut his throat. You and Izzy were gone by the time the other officers arrived."

The news knocked him backward. "What? But the Witch followed me into the woods. Who would have slit his throat?"

A firm knock caused them both to jump. Anna peered out of the side window to see who was at the door.

"Eric," she said. "Someone must have seen you walking over here. What do you want me to do?"

"I have nothing to hide," he replied.

He still hadn't fully processed the facts that Izzy had gone missing and the man who was hired to protect them had been murdered. Death had filled his day, something he would have nightmares about for years, but this was more personal, and the thought of something happening to Izzy caused a pain deep down in his stomach.

Anna opened the cottage door wide, putting Oliver's thin frame in Eric's eyeshot. The two said nothing at first. Part of Oliver still feared being blamed for the attacks. After all, he had been present for every single one except for Madeline's. The connection was an obvious one to make. *Still, how could I have flipped a police cruiser?*

"Is Izzy with you?" Eric asked, breaking the silence. His tone was that of legitimate concern.

"No. I was chased into the woods. I told her to lock herself in her room, and that was the last I saw of her."

"We haven't seen her since last night. We think she may have been taken. When the call from Ben came through, he mentioned something about a woman, said things were floating in the air. What the hell happened at Izzy's?"

"Everything he said was true," Oliver replied. "This woman, she's the one behind the attacks. Somehow, Simon's been controlling her. He's been using the carvings on the door to mark his target. I don't know why he's killing them, but he dropped this along the way, and he's been trying to track it down." Oliver pulled the Briarwood coin from his pocket. "Do you still have him in custody?"

The expression on Eric's face was a mixture of confusion and worry. "After the break-in, we let him go, told him to leave town."

Oliver's brow furrowed. "He killed Ben."

"We had no other evidence to keep him. The only thing linking him to the attack was a single sighting. We had no choice. What's so important about the damned coin?"

"The coin provides safe passage through the briars. It's a key and Simon's only ticket home."

Eric cocked his head.

"I know this sounds crazy. I have a hard time believing it myself, but I can show you if you take me there. I can guarantee Simon has Izzy, and he's not going to leave town until he has this coin. He's nearby."

Eric stepped outside to radio the station. Oliver

could only hope Simon hadn't already done away with Izzy and needed her for leverage to retrieve the coin.

Eric guided Oliver into the passenger seat of the cruiser. Oliver pulled his overcoat tightly around himself, careful not to reveal the weapon strapped to his waist.

The back door of the cruiser opened and shut behind him, and he turned to find Anna buckling herself in.

"You don't think I'm just going to sit this one out, do you?" she asked. "Just sit at home and wait? I don't think so."

CHAPTER TWENTY-FIVE

The cruiser cut across the field, wheels dipping in and out of the divots of uneven ground and weeds bending under its bumper. The periodic rain had caused the ground to soften, making the journey even more difficult.

"Can't believe I'm doing this," Eric said, gripping the steering wheel tightly as it jerked in his hands.

"Eric, you out there?" A voice came over the radio, slightly obscured by static.

"Go ahead," he replied.

"We just got a strange call from someone asking for you, claiming they had information about the attacks around town."

"Who?"

"That's the thing. They didn't say but claimed to

be calling from the Brighton place, on the edge of the woods."

"Lilly Brighton's place?"

"That's the one."

"We're headed in that general direction," Eric said. "Go ahead and send a few cars that way."

Despite the severity of the attacks on the town, the police force still held to its small-town informality—no coded language, just officers talking like everyday people.

"It's Simon," Oliver said. "It has to be."

"We'll stop by and check it out." Eric turned in the direction of the Brighton cabin. The drive would take them only a few minutes, assuming the car didn't bottom out or get stuck in a patch of mud.

The cabin sat just as it had when Anna and Oliver found the etching on the front door. The caution tape that had been strung across the entryway hung loosely from one side and fluttered in the wind. The cruiser's wheels spun slightly as it pulled up onto the gravel lot, spitting pebbles into the field behind it.

"Stay—" Eric started, but the door to the cabin opened before he had the chance to finish.

Izzy appeared in the doorway, wearing the same bright muumuu she'd had the night before. She was dirty and bruised, and her hair blew haphazardly in front of her eyes. A thin silver blade was pressed against her neck, drawing just the slightest amount of blood. As she stepped onto the front porch, Oliver could see the blade was attached to the handle of a cane, the same one he had seen in the bakery. Simon stood pressed up against her, staying in line with her silhouette and careful not to expose any part of his body, aside from the gloved hand holding the slender sword to Izzy's throat.

When Oliver gripped the car's door handle, Eric reached across to stop him. "Stay," he said.

Eric pressed the Talk button on the radio. "We have a hostage situation at the Brighton place."

He stepped out of the cruiser before receiving a response from dispatch. As he stood, he held a hand out toward Simon to tell him to wait. Simon was small and nearly powerless, a fraction of the man who had strutted into the bakery that day. This was an act of desperation, his last chance to reclaim the coin and return to the town that had once lived in fear of him and the Witch who murderously maintained his rule. From the looks of it, Izzy had put up a fight. One side of Simon's face was black and blue. His top hat was gone, and wisps of hair that had once been combed over to cover the man's balding head were blowing back and forth in the breeze.

Eric climbed out of the driver's seat and shut the

door behind him. As he stepped toward the cabin, Simon pulled Izzy back into the doorway.

Oliver knew Simon wouldn't leave the cabin without the key and stepped out of the vehicle.

"Oliver!" Simon shouted. "I want to speak to Oliver."

His voice strained against the wind as thunder rolled overhead and the sky started to drizzle once again. "Not you. You stay away. I want him, or else I slit her throat."

Eric looked back toward the cruiser.

"Let me speak with him," Oliver said to Eric.

Eric reluctantly stepped aside and cleared the way for Oliver to approach the cabin.

"How did you know we would be here?" Oliver asked.

"The police radio, you fool," Simon replied. "Now, show me the coin."

Oliver reached into his pocket and held the coin up in the air.

"Good," Simon replied. "Now drive the car over here. We're going for a little ride."

"I can't let you," Eric said.

"You have no choice," Simon replied, pressing himself closer to Izzy. "Now, bring the car closer to the porch."

Oliver looked at Eric, who shook his head.

"I will kill her!" Simon screamed. The blade had drawn more blood, which started to trickle down Izzy's throat.

"It's okay," Izzy said. It was the first time she had spoken since emerging from the cabin, but her voice was strong and resolute. "If he needs me that badly, he won't hurt me."

"Just get back in the car, and wait for me," Eric said.

Oliver climbed back inside and shut the door.

"What are we going to do?" Anna asked.

"You're going to get out of the car, and I'm going to drive it over to Simon," Oliver said, looking at the keys Eric had left in the ignition.

"What? Are you nuts?"

"Either you get out now, or you're coming with me. Time's running out."

"Drive, then. I'm not going anywhere," Anna replied.

He wished she'd left her hotheadedness back at the cottage. "There's a good chance that I may not come back. Now, get out of the car!"

Anna crossed her arms and looked ahead.

"Fine, then."

The sound of clicking door locks caught Eric's attention, and a look of horror crept across his face as Oliver climbed into the driver's seat.

He turned the key in the ignition and cracked the window. "He's going to make me drive into the woods. Watch the car and wait for me where it crosses!" he yelled before pulling away.

When Oliver pulled the cruiser closer to the porch, Simon thrust Izzy aside before climbing into the backseat.

"What is she doing here?" Simon asked.

"She's coming with us," Oliver replied. "Tried to talk her out of it, but she didn't budge." In truth, he was glad Anna was there—glad he didn't have to do this alone. Still, his comfort wasn't worth risking her life, but she was giving him no choice.

"Very well. Now, take me to the briars. If you turn away, if you make one wrong move, I will kill her."

Oliver looked in the rearview mirror and saw Simon's cane sword pressed against Anna's side.

Eric ran toward the car but only managed to slap the back of the trunk as it pulled away. He and Izzy grew smaller in the rearview mirror until their tiny specks disappeared completely.

Oliver wasn't sure what Simon had in mind. *Is he going to take the coin and flee? Will he actually let us live?*

When Oliver reached the edge of the woods, he looked back at Simon. "What do you want me to do?" he asked.

"Keep driving," he replied. The trees at the edge of the forest were sparse enough to allow the car to glide between them. The ride was rough, but they soon found themselves facing the briars, the patch that separated this world from the next.

"Through them!" Simon said, angry Oliver had lifted his foot off the gas.

Will the car be able to bring us all across safely? He wasn't sure if the coin worked in that way—hadn't had time to think about it—but he had little choice but to accelerate. If they did cross the threshold into the other world, it may very well be for the last time, for surely Simon wouldn't permit them to return. The realization washed over him. He had given the mysterious man in blue exactly what he wanted, and now it was too late to turn back. He looked back at Anna, but she only stared ahead with an expression of determination on her face. He held out some hope that his friends would be waiting on the other side, ready and willing to bring Simon to his knees for good.

A bank of trees lay opposite the patch, and the Witch appeared in front of them, hunched next to a stack of bodies. With no other purpose than to locate the coin—Oliver assumed—she must have stayed and waited for its return.

The sinewy vines crumpled under the wheels of the police car, providing no resistance. He pressed the pedal as far as it would go, bottoming out on the floor. He thought he might be able to hit her, to end all this.

"What are you doing? Slow down," Simon said.

Oliver didn't respond.

"I said slow down! You're going to hit the trees!"

Oliver reached up and pulled the seat belt down over himself as the car cleared the patch. He could see Anna was already buckled in, but Simon hadn't bothered.

The Witch sat waiting, guarding the entrance to the patch, surrounded by the remains of the hunting party. The car raced toward her, and as it passed through the invisible barrier, she lifted her head in response to the sound of the roaring engine. At that point, Simon was screaming, pleading for him to stop. He seemed to care more about slamming into the trees on the other side of the Witch than doing any harm to the Witch herself. He had dropped the sword, completely forgetting about his hostage.

CHAPTER TWENTY-SIX

Oliver braced himself for impact, throwing his hands in front of his face, closing his eyes, and preparing for the worst. The car bounced as it hit the edge of the patch, and just before its front tires slammed back down to earth, it stopped, causing everyone in the cab to lurch forward. Oliver slowly opened his eyes. An invisible force was holding the car suspended in the air and its occupants frozen in place. He could see the Witch past his crossed arms, standing there and peering inside the cab with her one good eye. Instead of tossing the car aside, as she had done with Ben's cruiser, she gingerly guided it to the ground with her gaze.

Simon took several moments to regain composure. Once the car was planted firmly on the ground, Simon picked up his weapon from the floorboards, opened the car door, and walked to the driver's side.

"You bastard!" he yelled, opening the door. Before Oliver could defend himself, Simon thrust the thin metal sword into his side. He twisted the handle, and searing pain shot up through Oliver's ribcage. "I ought to kill you now," he said. "But I'm not quite done with you yet." He pulled the sword from Oliver's side and brought it to his neck. "But if you try anything else, I won't hesitate to kill your friend. Now, get out!"

Although the blow seemed to have missed his vital organs, hitting only the fleshy part on the side of his torso, the pain still made Oliver grit his teeth. Growing impatient, Simon grabbed him by the collar and attempted to pull him out of the car, but he was too weak to do so.

The Witch ran to Simon like a dog running to its master. He slid his weapon back into his cane sheath. She sat at his feet, and he looked down at her with disdain.

"What are you waiting for?" he yelled, slapping the side of his cane against her cheek. "Get the boy out of the car. We're going home."

She recoiled from the sudden smack and pressed one of her hands against her face, the dirty yellowed fingernails a splash of color against her pale skin.

"Go, I said!" This time, he jabbed the cane into her ribcage.

Oliver felt the same force he had felt before, centered in his body, lifting him out of the seat. As he regained his footing, he looked toward the car, where Anna was still sitting in the backseat. After setting him upright, the Witch flicked her wrist in Anna's direction, releasing her invisible grip. The back passenger door flung open, and Anna was forcefully removed, with a look of panic still on her face.

The man who had cowered behind Izzy in the cabin was gone. His desperation had been replaced with unearned bravado, and he walked with the regal gait of a divine ruler. Something about his step was different, though. When Simon had come to the bakery to reclaim the coin, he hadn't bothered to use his cane, but now he seemed to depend on it. He'd played the feeble old man before, but now he wasn't acting and appeared to be growing weaker.

The procession marched through the edge of the forest, Simon followed by Oliver and Anna, with the Witch beside them, who had returned to her apelike crawl. The Witch had seemed so powerful before, but something about the way Simon treated her made Oliver feel a small pang of sympathy. She was indeed a full-grown woman, but she acted childlike around

Simon. He wondered how she'd developed her odd crawl and lost her eye, having seen Simon cane her. Her humanity had clearly been beaten out of her, and she served only to do her master's—her father's—bidding. If he treated his own daughter like this, he must have been brutal to the townspeople. But as with any cruel master of a slave, he was powerless without her obedience.

Oliver's movement was restricted, as if he were surrounded by a glass bubble. When he started to stray too far from the pack, the invisible walls kept him in line. Simon hadn't noticed the weapon in Oliver's belt. *If only I could reach it without being noticed.* They walked past the center of the square, where he had once stood bound to a wooden stake, then past the dark storefronts of the ragtag revolutionaries who had cut him loose, risking their own lives to save his. He wondered where they were and hoped they were devising another last-minute salvation, a final plot to overthrow the grand puppeteer who strode so confidently in front of him.

Oliver looked to his left then his right. While some of the citizens started to gather, spewing from the stores, others hid inside, pulling blinds and latching doors. A few fell to their knees, clasping their hands together and overcome with the realization that their protector had returned. Still, no one came close to him, not even within a few feet, because everyone knew to avoid the Witch. None had likely seen her in the daylight before, but she was the unifying factor between the loyalists and the rebels—she punished both equally.

Simon stopped in front of the toppled statue, kneeling next to the twisted metal that had once been Nathaniel Hale.

"So I leave for a moment," he said, "and this is what they do? This is how they repay my family for all we've done? For hundreds of years of protection?" He massaged his temples.

"Looks like I've got some work to do," he said, forcing the corners of his mouth into a sickening smile.

Oliver wondered where the revolution had gone. So many had been waiting for a chance to topple Simon's rule as they had toppled the statue in the town square, but they were nowhere to be found. *Why hadn't they taken advantage of the opportunity?*

"These are the lights you saw in the woods, aren't they?" Anna broke his concentration. "This town has been here this whole time? How could we have missed it?"

"The coin," Oliver replied. "You have to possess the coin in order to be able to see this place—in order to be able to cross the patch. Simon must have dropped it when he etched the symbol on Francis's door."

"Got the dropsies do you, big boy?" Anna shot the snide comment in Simon's direction, but the man ignored her and focused instead on the town hall across the square.

The building stood unguarded, and they strolled up the front steps, meeting no resistance along the way. Oliver had only seen the inside of the meeting hall, but the room seemed stark in comparison to the elegant atrium, which held a grand marble staircase and portraits of who he assumed were the descendants of the town founder. Light swirled in the atrium above them, a blend of oranges and yellows casting a sunset glow over the room. The proportions of the structure seemed impossible. The building must have extended several floors above the atrium, but he hadn't noticed the domed ceiling from the outside. The light wasn't coming from the sun, either. The source must have been man-made.

"What is this place?" Anna asked.

"This is where we handle all town business, but it also happens to be my home," Simon replied. Instead of crossing the hall, he turned toward a staircase along the right wall. After climbing the first set of steps, they took another until they reached a long, paneled hallway.

"I have to take certain precautions," he continued, "for some feel my policies are a bit harsh." He pressed the end of his cane against the wall, causing a panel to shift backward and slide out of the way, revealing a small spiral staircase behind it. "But there is a certain price we must all pay for security. I have to keep the town safe from people like you."

"What are you talking about?" Oliver replied.

"Outsiders," he said.

"It's your fault we're here." Oliver was growing angry. "You murdered three people. For what? For security?"

Simon laughed. "No, not security. I simply thought it was time the people who run that damned town pay for what they did to my family. Thought the three-hundred-year anniversary would be a nice time to remind them we haven't forgotten, and who better to target than the old hags who pull the strings?"

The top of the staircase led to a large platform. They were level with the mysterious source of light swirling above the atrium. Oliver couldn't see the ceiling above them, nor walls for that matter. The edges of the room disappeared into the darkness, but he was certain they were still inside.

The domed glass had been a false window after all and formed the bottom of a curved pool containing some sort of colorful liquid. Whatever circulated in the pool seemed to defy gravity, flowing up and over the crest of the dome, with no discernible path nor pattern. A narrow bridge extended from the platform to the peak of the dome, which contained a metal apparatus that extended into the liquid below. The contraption reminded Oliver of the old-fashioned air-pressure tubes bank tellers used to use to send documents back and forth at the bank drive-through.

"What is it?" he asked.

"It's power," Simon answered without giving the question any thought.

A large metal door jutted from the ground like a jagged tooth protruding from the mouth of an old man. The frame was oddly shaped, one side perpendicular to the floor, with the other slanted at an odd angle. Like the exterior lantern room that hung from the building, the door was plated with corroded copper. Cast-iron gears lined its surface, forming an odd clockwork tapestry that reminded Oliver of the Clockmaker's elegant grandfather clocks. The door was bordered by a set of glass tubes, which seemed to be filled with the same liquid that circulated in the pool behind it.

"You like it?" Simon asked. "It was built by our town's very own clockmaker. Took him ages."

Oliver hadn't noticed it from a distance, but the door's copper surface was stamped with a small honey-comb pattern. Thousands of tiny copper cells extended from top to bottom. Without a second glance, Simon pressed the tip of his cane into one of the hexagons, pushed and twisted. A few of the gears spun, and a metal handle extended from the door's surface. He turned it, entering a careful sequence of positions like a combination lock, before returning it to its original position and pressing it back into the door.

The door didn't have a seam, but as the gears came to life, they started to shift away from the center. The small copper pieces resembled scales undulating in three-dimensional space as they overlapped and moved outward, leaving a small person-sized portal where copper had once been.

Simon ushered the group through the doorway, and just as he started to insert the tip of his cane in a groove on the other side, a voice echoed through the atrium room.

"Sir! Wait! It's me!"

This startled the Witch, who spun round, momentarily releasing her invisible grip on Oliver and Anna.

As Elias emerged from the darkness, grasping at his throat, Oliver inched his hand toward the weapon in his belt. A swift crack of Simon's cane to Oliver's side sent him to the floor, reeling in pain.

"Let's not make this any harder than it has to be," Simon said. "Let him go. It's Elias, you twit!" he said to the Witch.

She released her grip on Elias, who stumbled forward, gasping for air.

Anna gave a death glare to Simon and knelt next to Oliver. She pulled his coat open and examined the gash in his blood-soaked shirt.

"Take his weapon off, and leave it on the ground," Simon said.

While Anna loosened Oliver's holster, Elias approached the door. "So happy to see you, sir. We were beginning to worry."

Anna helped Oliver to his feet, and Elias bent down to pick up the weapon.

"And who are our guests?"

"Visitors from beyond the patch," Simon said.

"I'm Oliver," he said through gritted teeth.

He watched Elias's reaction carefully as a glint of recognition in the man's eyes was quickly snuffed by a nervous gulp. Although Elias had only met Oliver in the darkness of the dungeon, he would surely recognize the name.

Something isn't right. Why would they release him?

Once inside the elaborate doorway, Simon inserted the tip of his cane into a groove on the other side and entered another secret combination. The shimmering scales slid back into place, closing the room off from the outside world. Two guards stood on either side of the door in front of them, long metal swords sheathed on one side of their belt and elaborate percussion pistols on the other. Compared to the weapon the Clockmaker had crafted in his workshop, these were children's toys.

A short man stumbled forward, surprised by Simon's return. "Oh, thank heavens," he said, rushing forward to take Simon's blue coat. "The staff was beginning to worry. We'll need to resupply soon."

"Resupply?" Anna asked.

"We keep enough up here to last us for weeks, if not months," Elias replied. "This place is completely self-sufficient, and no one gets in or out without Master's key."

Elias must have been locked out since Simon's departure and spent most of that time in the dungeon. Oliver still wasn't sure why he was walking free now, but he dared not say anything.

The man took Simon's coat and disappeared behind the door to the left of the entryway. Simon walked forward, and one of the guards opened the center door for him. The room was filled with the late-afternoon sun sneaking through the cracks of receding storm clouds. Oliver had seen the lantern room from the outside, but the inside was much larger than he'd imagined. The front walls were lined with bookshelves stacked upon a sleek wooden floor that had been waxed to a fine sheen. The back held a grand desk, which extended into the lantern portion of the room that jutted out over the town below. Copper spiraled down the rain-speckled panes of glass, holding them securely in place. A chandelier hung from the ceiling, but the typical glass panels were replaced by polished metal, and the light from a large central flame bounced off them, casting a flickering glow over the entire space.

Oliver was struck by the room's beauty. In the brief moment he had to examine the books on the shelves, he noticed that most seemed out of place. While the town had shown few signs of modernity, a few of these books were new. The shelves contained books on English, history, business, and other random topics, and it seemed the *glorious leader* must have brought some back from his adventures across the patch. No wonder he was able to blend in with the people of Christchurch, garish suit aside.

Elias nervously checked his pocket watch. "I'll take her to her room and ensure she receives dinner," he said, snapping his fingers at the Witch.

"Tend to her wounds." Simon opened his desk drawer and pulled out two small glass vials. He threw one to Elias then twisted the body of his cane and poured the contents of the other into a small spout that appeared in the center. *The red paint on the doors.*

"Oh, take them too. Let them spend a little time

together before we hang them in the square," he added without emotion.

Oliver's stomach dropped. "But we helped you—gave you the key that brought you back here."

"Oh, thank you for reminding me—the coin please." Simon held out his palm.

Oliver pulled the coin from his pocket and handed it to Simon.

"You've made my life quite difficult—I think you know that. I can't let you go. No, I have bigger plans for you. Hanging a few murderous outsiders should help to restore some order around here. We'll make up a nice story to go along with it too."

"Let her go," Oliver said. "I'll do whatever you want if you let her go back home. You can keep me."

"The time for bargaining is over," Simon replied. "You have no more cards to play. Now, take them away."

Elias led them to a cell-like room just off the entryway to the lantern room. Anna was holding back tears as the Witch crawled into the chamber like a puppy returning to her training crate.

The light from Simon's office illuminated the interior of the cell. The bottom half of the cell walls were covered with crude chalk drawings. At first, they appeared childlike and innocent, but the more he looked, the more the smiley faces reminded him of the

Witch's victims, mouths stretched inhumanly wide. *She was trying to make them smile.*

Elias pointed toward the far corner of the room, where Anna and Oliver sat on the floor. He held one of the manacles up and shook it, rattling the chains and capturing the Witch's attention. She crawled to him, and he secured her to the floor. *No wonder she's barely able to walk.*

"Let's see what they've done to you," Elias said, twisting the dropper out of the small vial of iridescent liquid. He pulled back the shoulder of the Witch's nightdress, revealing the crusted bullet wound underneath.

"It's good for everything," he said while filling the dropper with liquid. "You may have noticed the street-lights? The lights in the town hall? The door? They're all powered by it."

He gripped the Witch's shoulder and pressed his thumb firmly into her wound, causing her to squeal and pull away.

"Now, now," he said. "We need to make sure it mixes with fresh blood."

A trickle of the Witch's blood ran down her shoulder, and Elias's hand shook as he extended the dropper to her wound.

"Why so nervous?" Oliver asked.

Elias shot a glance in his direction but ignored the

question. He pulled the Witch's hair back and added another few drops to the gash on the side of her head. The scene brought flashbacks of Oliver's childhood, his mother dabbing alcohol onto a scraped knee. Elias must have been the closest person the Witch had to a caretaker.

The bullet wound on the Witch's shoulder was probably a half inch in diameter, and the blood around the gash began to bubble. The wound itself started to fill as the serum expanded like some sort of grotesque foam.

"There we are," Elias said. His face had grown pale, and Oliver noticed a bead of sweat running down his forehead.

"Mind throwing some of that my way?" Oliver asked.

Elias let out a nervous chuckle and tossed the vial in Oliver's direction. "Have at it. I have nothing left to lose."

Anna looked at Oliver with raised eyebrows.

Elias closed the door and placed a wooden plank across the doorframe, causing a loud clunk as the bar shifted into place. If not for the light sneaking through the edges of the door, they would have been in complete darkness.

Oliver lifted his shirt, which had been soaked in crimson. The gash had glazed over with a thin layer of coagulated blood. It would certainly need stitches. He pressed into it and winced as a bright red seeped through the scab. The remaining liquid trickled from the dropper into Oliver's open wound and was followed by an intense burning sensation.

"What are you doing?" Anna whispered. "You don't know what that stuff is."

"If he's going to hang us in the square, it won't matter much, will it? Besides, we'll have a much better chance of figuring a way out if we're both in good shape. The townspeople have got to be up to something—I know it. They wouldn't just let him take the town over again without a fight." The more time passed, the less Oliver was certain anyone would be coming for them, but he was trying to keep Anna optimistic.

"I'm so sorry," he said. "I shouldn't have let you come with me."

"Don't you get it?" she snapped. "Not everything is up to you, Oliver. I chose to come. We're like family, and we're going to figure a way out of this together."

"I'm sorry."

"Stop apologizing, and help me think through this," she replied.

A small panel slid open at the bottom of the door, and a plate of food slid through. The Witch scurried to the dish and scooped food into her mouth.

"How long do you think it's been since she's eaten?" Anna asked.

"No telling," he replied.

Once the Witch had finished, she pushed the plate toward the door and retreated to the corner. An eerie tune filled the cell, a high-pitched hum accompanied by the sound of chalk scraping against the cell wall.

CHAPTER TWENTY-SEVEN

Shouting pulled Oliver from a paranoid dream. He and Anna had been leaning on each other when the sound jolted him awake. A crash followed, sounding as if someone had ripped Simon's office door off its hinges.

Oliver's heart raced, but the initial feelings of fear were replaced by relief. "They're coming for Simon," he whispered.

Anna gripped Oliver hard. "Are we safe?"

"They're going to save us," he replied. "They must have seen us when we walked through town. That's why they let Elias loose. It was a trap."

The viewing window slid open, causing Oliver to squint from the sudden burst of light. He heard the heavy wooden bar sliding loose, but before he had time to warn the person on the other side about the Witch, the door creaked open.

Gideon's silhouette appeared in the doorway, and a group of men stood behind him.

As his eyes adjusted and light filled the room, Oliver saw the Witch curled up on the floor, chest slowly rising and falling. *How can she sleep through this?*

Gideon leaned over and helped Anna and Oliver to their feet.

The men moved to one side, clearing the path to Simon's office. Mercy stood next to Simon's desk, and Elias sat on the floor, hands bound behind his back.

"How did you get in?" Oliver asked.

Mercy gestured toward Elias.

Elias scowled. "You promised me," he said. "Now, where is it?" His voice was low and agitated.

Mercy pulled a glass vial from her pocket and popped the stopper. She held it to Elias's lips and tipped it back until the algae-colored liquid dripped, syrup-like, into his mouth.

"What is that?" Oliver asked.

"An antidote. Had to keep him honest. Promised the vial if he helped open the door," Mercy replied.

"But how'd you get in without the cane?"

"I happen to know the man who designed the key. We just needed someone who knows the combination, and fortunately Elias here has seen Hale open the door a few thousand times. He was also kind enough to slip something special into the Witch's supper, just in case. Couldn't have her running about while we tried to break in. She'll rest for a while longer, but we need to be quick. We have to find Simon before he slips away. Grab your weapon, and let's be on our way!" Mercy stepped aside, revealing the gun belt Simon had taken from him earlier. "Take it."

"But it's yours. Don't you want it back?"

"I'll be fine with the daggers. We've cleared the guards. Now, take it, and let's go."

Oliver strapped on the belt as the group entered the hallway. Across from him stood the portal, still wide open, and two guards lay hunched in the corner next to it.

"You"—Mercy pointed at Anna—"stay here and watch the portal with Aymes."

"The name's Anna," Anna added.

"All right then—*Anna*, stay here and watch the portal with Aymes."

Mercy opened the door to the left of the portal, and Oliver and Gideon followed closely behind. They were greeted by a white-wainscoted dining room with tall ceilings and an elegantly carved mahogany table sitting atop a red Persian rug.

"This must be Simon's private residence," Mercy said.

The wall sconces housed the same irregular flame as the massive lantern in Simon's office, and the flickering light bounced off the silverware that had been laid out in carefully constructed patterns on the table. They walked through the dining room and into another large foyer.

"How big is this place?" Oliver looked up at the flying staircase, which led up to yet another floor.

"Spread out." Mercy pulled the two daggers from her belt. "We'll check the other rooms down here, and you head upstairs," she told Oliver.

Oliver ascended the suspended staircase to the upper floor while the others explored the rooms on the first. Like the town itself, the building's existence seemed impossible based on the view from the outside. The tall foyer and winding hallways extended far past the boundaries of the hall visible to the naked eye. Some sort of magic must have surrounded the place, making it appear smaller than it actually was.

A cracked door caught his attention. While all the others had been closed, this one had been left ajar. As he approached, he clenched his fist around the grip of the gun sword and pulled it from the belt. He wasn't exactly sure what he'd be able to do with it if confronted, but he felt a sense of security with it in his hand.

Reassurance came in the form of Gideon's heavy step on the landing behind him. He held a broadsword, the same he'd pulled from the rice barrel, in attack position. Although Oliver was panicked, sweaty, and pale, Gideon showed no signs of worry. He exuded gallant confidence, so much that Oliver could almost feel it in the air surrounding him.

Mercy approached from behind. "The first floor is empty," she said.

The door led to a long hallway, lit—once again—by the odd-colored flames. *If this isn't gas, what is it? Elias said it powered the whole town.* The glow from the flames flickered against the maroon-and-burgundy-striped wallpaper, lighting the faces in the portraits lining the walls. Large wooden double doors sat at the end of the hallway. Oliver turned the elaborate gold handles, but they were locked tight. A small hexagonal indentation sat where a keyhole would normally go. Just like the large clockwork door that protected Simon's residence from the outside world, this one was meant to be opened only by the tip of Simon's cane.

Oliver felt a hand on his shoulder, and when he turned, Gideon gestured for him to move aside. With two sweeping motions, Gideon lifted his foot into the air and drove it into the middle of the doors. The wood cracked and splintered around the latch at the center, sending both doors flying open and clearing the way to enter the room.

Oliver looked over at Gideon, who cocked his head to one side as if to say "go ahead." He entered the room slowly, checking the corners in case Simon was hiding in wait, but a part of him didn't expect the man to attack. If his experience with Simon had taught him anything, it was that Simon was a coward.

The room appeared to be a master bedroom and was built with the same extravagant touches as Simon's office. The edges of the tall paneled ceiling were gilded, and a fire roared in the large fireplace. The silk sheets of the four-poster bed had been turned down in anticipation of their owner's return, and a blanket of animal fur lined the foot of the bed.

Oliver passed a writing desk, on which sat an antique globe. The continents were familiar but were slightly skewed and inaccurate. It reminded Oliver of Simon's view of the world. Although the man might have crossed over the briar patch many times and had been exposed to life outside of the town, his mind was still a product of Briarwood and the tangential history the town had created for itself.

As Oliver's eyes rose from the globe, they landed on a small slit in the wallpaper on the opposing wall. The split was subtle, just visible along the edge of the bookcase standing beside it. He traced the line with his eyes, and it extended three-quarters of the way up then turned at a right angle and disappeared behind the bookcase.

"Look at this," he called to the other two, who had been searching the other side of the room. Oliver ran a finger along the edge of the bookcase as Gideon watched. Gideon gripped the edge of the bookshelf and pulled. The shelf appeared to be fixed to the wall and was slightly suspended, gliding above the hardwood floor underneath as Gideon opened the secret door.

The room on the other side was tiny, just the size of a closet, but it held the entrance of a cast-iron spiral staircase that extended into the floor below.

CHAPTER TWENTY-EIGHT

The platform at the bottom of the stairs led to another cell, separated by a thick wooden door with a small cross-hatched window. Mercy pushed the door open and entered the dungeonlike room on the other side.

Oliver stepped through the open door and into the chamber. The small barred window let in just enough moonlight to illuminate the objects next to it. Bookcases lined the stone walls, filled to the brim with books of various shapes and sizes. Oliver's eyes scanned the room until they settled on the outline of a body slumped in a wooden chair. Blood formed intricate patterns down both the man's arms, much like the tangled mess of briars that surrounded the town. This blood was different, though, somehow phosphorescent in the dark room. The man looked to be no more than Oliver's age.

An overturned wooden bowl sat at the figure's feet, splotched with the same liquid that lined the man's arms. Oliver thought back to the pool on top of the atrium filled with the same swirling colors. The same stuff had fueled the lanterns in the square and healed the deep gash in his side.

The town is powered by blood.

A small metal box, about two inches long on each side, sat on the wooden table next to the body. Long metal slits interlaced with each other on the front, and a short lever protruded from the back.

"What is that?" Oliver asked.

"It draws blood to help with illness," Mercy replied. "The box is filled with small metal blades that cut the skin. I've seen the doctor use it before. But why would someone do this to him?"

Oliver knelt next to the figure slumped in the chair. Upon closer inspection, he could see the man's arms were covered in several sets of small slits, as if someone had taken the contraption and used it over and over again.

A soft groan rose from the man's lips, startling Oliver.

"He's still alive!" Oliver turned to face Gideon. "We have to get him out of here. Help me carry him."

"I can't let you do that," Simon said from the shadows.

Gideon turned, lifting his weapon to strike, but Mercy was standing between him and Simon, Simon's hand wrapped around her neck and a revolver pressed against her ribcage. The weapon wasn't like Oliver's—it looked as if Simon had brought it back from one of his trips across the briars.

"Wouldn't do that," Simon said.

Gideon held the blade in the air, as if contemplating whether he could bring the sword down on Simon's head before the man could pull the trigger. After a few moments, Gideon loosened his grip, brought the sword down slowly, and rested it at his side.

As Simon stepped out of the shadows, his face no longer obscured by darkness, Oliver noticed the man's lips were outlined with the same glowing liquid that ran from the man's arms. A dribble of blood ran from the corner of his mouth and down his stubbled chin. Simon's face was pulsating, as if small insects were scurrying underneath his skin, and the wrinkles lining his forehead had slowly started to disappear.

"You're a monster," Oliver said.

"Oh, he'll be fine in a few minutes. Have to say I'm a bit embarrassed to be found in such a sorry state, but it had been a while, and I was starting to feel my age slowly creep back up on me. It doesn't quite stop the aging process, but it sure does put a spring back in my step," Simon replied, as if he'd been talking about a protein shake, and his cold nonchalance mixed with his bloodstained face made him appear truly, deeply evil.

Simon walked over to the chair, keeping the pistol aimed at Mercy. He gave the man in the chair a swift kick in the shin, which seemed to pull him out of his daze.

Oliver noticed the marks on his arm had healed over, leaving barely visible scars, lines of raised skin that were slightly lighter than the rest. His arm was covered with dozens of the tiny little marks, as though the tool had been used on him hundreds of times before.

He shook his head and slowly slid out of the chair and onto his feet. He clearly had been too delirious to notice the two others in the room, but as Simon pulled the man past them, he looked at them with innocent curiosity.

"Who are these people, Father?" he asked.

Father?

Oliver recalled Mercy's story of the oxygen-starved baby and her brother who died in early childhood. Her brother hadn't died after all.

"Wait by the staircase, you twit," Simon snapped.

The man stumbled forward as he regained his footing and left the room.

"I assure you, you all are going to get what you want. I will leave. You can have your little town, and all that I'll take is the boy," Simon said in an eerie singsong voice. He spoke as if he still had some control over the situation although Oliver hoped the other rebels were closing in on the room above them.

As Oliver stepped toward the spiral staircase, Simon aimed the pistol at him. "You just stay put for now," he said. "I'm sure your friends will find you soon enough." He pulled Mercy toward the door, shifting his grip to her hair in order to keep hold of her through the cross-hatched window. The large wooden bolt slid into place on the other side of the door.

Where does Simon plan to take him? There's nowhere to run.

A staccato gunshot echoed through the chamber, causing Oliver's ears to ring. Mercy let out a surprised gasp and fell forward.

As Simon started to climb the staircase, metal steps clinking under his feet, he turned back. "Do you think I'd just walk away? Let you take everything I've worked for without so much as a whimper? How foolish you truly are." He began to spit with anger. "I'd kill the two of you, too, if I didn't think I'd need the goddamn bullets. But I'll be back—for you, for Christchurch, and for Briarwood."

Oliver was stunned, and by the time he pulled his weapon and aimed through the window, Simon had already ascended the staircase and was out of sight.

He rushed toward Mercy, who had a single gunshot wound on the left side of her chest.

"Help me roll her over," Oliver told Gideon.

They turned Mercy onto her back, but she was limp and unresponsive.

"Come on, Mercy," he said, slapping her lightly on the cheek. He tried to feel for a pulse but found none although he had no clue whether or not he was checking in the right spot.

Oliver's heart raced as he tried to think of a way to save her. He looked over at the overturned wooden bowl, still stained with the iridescent blood.

"We've got to find some of his blood," he said, scrambling over to grab the bowl. The vessel looked as if Simon had licked it clean, and he managed to gather only a small amount on his fingertips.

Without waiting for Gideon, Oliver struggled to turn Mercy over onto her stomach. He wiped the bowl again with his fingers then pressed them against her wound. He waited for something—any sign that Mercy was still alive—but her body remained still, and the glowing liquid did little more than fizzle around the edges of the bullet wound.

"It's not working." Oliver stumbled over his words as tears filled the corners of his eyes.

The statement seemed to send Gideon over the edge. He ran toward the cell door, slamming his shoulder into it. Although he had easily been able to break the doors into Simon's bedroom, this one was much sturdier. He tried again, but it held firm, secured by the thick wooden plank on the other side. After punching the door hard in exasperation, he paced to the other side of the room and overturned one of the bookcases.

"Oliver?" A familiar voice echoed down the staircase and through the chamber.

"We're down here!" he yelled.

Anna descended the staircase and peered through the small window in the cell door.

"Oh my God," she said when she noticed Mercy's crumpled form on the floor. She pulled the heavy wooden bar out of the way and pulled the door open.

Gideon walked toward the door and knelt next to Mercy.

"Take her, and I'll find Simon," Oliver said, placing a hand on Gideon's shoulder.

Gideon lifted her up into a fireman's carry, pushed past Anna, and climbed the staircase.

"Is she...?" Anna asked.

Oliver locked eyes with Anna but was unable to say the words. Instead, he marched past her and toward the staircase. "Where's Simon?"

"I don't know, but there are even more people here now. They've come to help."

When they reached Simon's bedroom, Oliver noticed a flipped table that had been sitting on top of an upturned corner of the large Persian rug. A small wooden hatch, just large enough for an average-sized man, was carved out of the floor where the rug had been.

"I have to go after him. Tell the others," Oliver said, sliding his feet into the open hatch.

"Wait, why?" Anna asked.

"He has the coin. If he crosses into Christchurch, we'll never be able to go back. We'll be trapped here." Oliver's head disappeared into the hatch.

"Well, at least wait for me," she added as she prepared to climb.

The tunnel was a straight shot down to the ground. They carefully worked their way down the aged wooden planks, occasionally breaking off rotted pieces into the abyss below. The tunnel must have been there for centuries, neglected over the years of unquestioned rule.

Chilly night air whipped against Oliver's back, and

moonlight shone through an opening at the base of the tunnel. A wooden door had been framed with stone and made to look like part of the building's foundation from the outside. He slid through the crack in the door and pulled it open for Anna.

Simon must have sneaked around the back of the building, where he would have been able to escape under cover of the woods.

"We have to go back to where we crossed in the car," Oliver said. "If they're crossing, that's where they'll do it." He grabbed Anna by the arm and tugged her toward the forest.

As they crossed the front of the building, they caught the attention of two townspeople standing guard next to the entryway.

"He's headed toward the briars. Tell the others!" Oliver yelled.

When they reached the edge of the woods, a loud explosion came from behind. Oliver turned to see glass pouring from the lantern-shaped room on the side of the town hall, raining down like glitter in the moonlight. A pale form emerged from the shattered window, torn nightgown billowing in the breeze.

"She's out. Somehow, she's gotten out," he wheezed.

"Better run faster, then," Anna panted.

Lightning crisscrossed the whirling storm clouds

overhead as Oliver and Anna arrived at the edge of the briars. Oliver caught a glimpse of Simon and the boy midpatch, thorns shifting around their feet.

"There's no way we're going to catch them," Oliver said.

"The cruiser," Anna replied. "Maybe we can catch up before they cross."

Oliver looked over at the police cruiser they'd crossed in earlier that day. "Come on," he said, but Anna was already halfway to the passenger side of the car.

The key jingled in the ignition as Oliver slammed the door. At first, the engine refused to turn, but with a few persistent twists of the key, it roared to life.

He turned the car around, and the headlights illuminated the briars. Simon and the boy had nearly cleared the patch. Another figure was perched at the edge of the woods, though. The Witch sat facing the briars, completely ignoring Oliver and Anna behind her. Her broken chains hung limp at her sides.

"Without the key, she's got no chance," Oliver said. The Witch seemed to know that too.

"What are you waiting for? Drive!" Anna said.

"There's a wall, some sort of barrier in the middle. Even if we can make it through the briars, we won't be able to clear the wall. It's too late."

"No, we have to try!" Anna grabbed for the wheel.

"Just hold on a minute. Look," Oliver said, pointing toward the patch.

Once Simon made it safely to the field, he turned back toward Briarwood. As he did, the Witch's head twitched to one side, and she rose to her feet. With hobbled steps, she entered the patch. The briars were quick to act, climbing her legs and working their way upward. At first, she pulled herself free, slowly making progress across the pit of vines. But as she stumbled deeper and deeper into the patch, the vines became more vicious and pulled her toward the ground. Once she fell to her knees, she was quickly consumed by a writhing sea of green.

Simon seemed to hesitate at first as if he were debating whether or not to turn back and help. Oliver was unsure if he paused because the Witch was his daughter or because he would lose a powerful weapon if he let the patch consumer her. Eventually, he turned and trudged across the field, leaving her behind.

Oliver heard a rustling in the woods behind him as a group of rebels approached, eager for their chance to bring the brutal leader to his knees. They stood for a moment, surveying the field ahead, but their collective expression shifted from one of disappointment to slack-jawed amazement. When Oliver turned to see what had caught their attention, he was greeted by a sea of blooming roses. As the vines tore into the Witch, her blood seemed to bring them to life. But with the blooms came something else. The pulse was small at first, a subtle shift in the vines where the Witch had disappeared. The patch seemed to have developed a heartbeat, but the motion grew more prominent, throbbing and swelling where the roses bloomed most brilliantly.

A blast came next, an explosion of snapped thorns and brambles. Oliver and Anna both instinctively shielded their eyes although they were protected by the car's windshield, which deflected the bits of debris flying toward them. The sudden explosion seemed to grab Simon's attention too, and he stopped and turned midway through the field.

The Witch lay in the center of a circle of bare earth with the vines around it blown backward and resembling a slipshod crown of thorns. She slowly pushed herself up to her hands and knees. Her body had been ripped and torn by thorns, and laces of blood appeared on her already-tattered clothing. She rose back onto her knees, not braced by her hands but rather by some invisible force that seemed to lift her toward the sky, just as she had lifted her victims. She flung her head back, black tangles of hair hanging freely, and her body rose upward until her feet no longer touched the ground.

The Witch glided through the air, her limbs positioned as if she were being crucified, arms outward and toes pointed toward the earth. The devastation seemed to follow her from below, ripping aside the branches that grasped at her feet, leaving a cleared trail in her wake.

When she reached the edge of the patch, she stopped as though sensing the invisible barrier. Simon stood and watched, the spectacle seemingly amusing to him. He was safely on the other side, and no amount of brute force could penetrate the wall. At least, that's what Oliver had assumed.

For a moment, the Witch hovered there, motionless except for the slight sway of her body in the wind. Occasionally, a vine or two would reach up toward her feet, but most had retreated, as if some sort of survival instinct was engrained in them. She stared across the field, and Oliver could see her brother, on the other side, staring back. He lifted an arm toward the patch, toward the Witch, who levitated on the other side, and she raised hers back. For a moment, Oliver held his breath, not sure what would happen next and completely forgetting about the revolutionaries who stood at the edge of the patch next to him. He wondered if the son had ever been permitted to leave his cell, to see his sister. *Did she even know he was still alive?*

Simon jerked him around, pulling him away from

the patch and toward the hill and Izzy's home. He was leaving the Witch behind. This seemed to upset her, and she let out a wail so loud that Oliver and Anna could hear it through the closed windows. She lifted her arms above her head, wrists casually crossing as if she were stretching. The loose debris from the patch below her feet began to float, just as the furniture in Izzy's house had during the attack the other night. Oliver swore he felt lighter, as though she were lifting the car too. When she brought her arms down, nothing happened at first. For a brief moment, the loose twigs and broken vines hung in the air, and then everything came crashing to the ground with a gust of violent wind. The trees above Oliver shook, sending a shower of leaves down upon the group. He looked up at the sky, and even the clouds appeared to have been pulled toward the Witch as a puffy stalactite formed in the center of the ominous storm.

Lightning cracked through the sky, striking the ground in front of the Witch. Oliver felt static in the air, and the sudden bolt caused the hair on his arms to stand on end. Instead of instantly dissipating, the bright plasma branches left a red-hot scar on the invisible wall separating Briarwood from the edges of Christchurch. He knew the barrier had been there, but this was the first time he was actually able to see it, outlined by the lightning strike.

As the Witch hovered toward Simon, the glowing scar on the dome grew. The lightning pattern branched off as if the barrier had been made of glass and was slowly starting to crack.

Bits of the barrier broke away and came down in a shimmering waterfall. As the pieces fell, erasing the separation between the two worlds, Izzy's house appeared in the distance, no longer obscured by the magic barrier. The dome didn't shatter completely—rather, the blast left a jagged portal in its side just large enough for a police cruiser.

"Buckle up," Oliver said, pulling his seatbelt over his shoulder. He shifted the car into drive and stepped on the gas. At first, the wheels spun in the soft mud, but the tires eventually gripped the earth and propelled the car forward.

The Witch had left a path behind, but the vines were spreading and covering the damaged area. He could hear the snapping of vines underneath the wheels, and eventually, the car began to struggle as the briars came for it.

Oliver looked up at the portal, their only hope of ever escaping Briarwood, and floored it. He didn't look back, didn't have time to say goodbye to those who had saved him—but if he ever had the chance, he would return the favor. The sharp edges of the portal began to smooth over, filling in the red cracks until they were transparent once again. The top of the car scraped against the jagged edges of the portal, but the cruiser managed to clear it, making it to the edge of the forest beyond the patch. By the time he looked in the rearview mirror, all that remained of the doorway were fading red skeletal outlines in the invisible wall. The car slid to a halt as he considered his next course of action.

Oliver wasn't sure what the Witch would do if she caught up with Simon or her brother, but he was now close enough to see the damage the thorns had done to her body. Deep gashes spiraled down her arms and legs, filled with blood and surrounded by puffy pink skin. The Witch seemed to pay the car no mind, though, and continued to float up the base of the hill toward Izzy's, picking up speed as she tried to catch up with Simon and the boy, who were now specks on the hill.

Something else escaped the Witch's attention, though—another police cruiser approaching from the direction of Lilly's cabin. Perhaps the officers inside had seen the lightning strike or heard the explosive boom that came with it. Oliver wasn't quite sure what exactly had led them there, but because he didn't have the Briarwood key, they had been invisible to him, obscured by the remnants of the barrier surrounding the hidden town.

As the rain poured, two officers emerged from the car with guns drawn. They stood in the crooks of their cruiser doors with looks of shock on their faces as they watched the Witch float above the field.

After several moments of dreadful silence, one of the officers shouted, "Stop!" The command seemed to reach the Witch's ears, but instead of halting, she merely flicked her wrist, sending the officer flying backward. The remaining officer opened fire, sending a spray of bullets toward her, ripping through her tattered gown into her pale flesh and causing her to fall to the ground.

"She'll kill them," Anna said. "We have to do something."

Oliver pressed the gas pedal to the floor and pointed the car directly at the Witch. She regained her footing and turned toward the other cruiser. With another flick of the wrist, she ripped the car sideways, sending it spinning like a pinwheel. As her invisible grip lifted the second officer in the air, Oliver's car barreled into her. The Witch flipped onto the hood and smashed into the windshield, body breaking the glass before flipping over the hood and back onto the ground. Anna screamed and lifted her arms to shield her eyes.

The Witch lay in the field behind him, and he felt sick to his stomach at the thought of what he'd just done. She was nothing more than an abused child, but he couldn't let her kill again. Oliver saw the second officer in his periphery. He'd fallen to his feet and was running to check his partner.

"We have to keep going," Oliver said, pulling himself together and straightening the wheel. "What if Izzy's home? He's headed straight for her."

He had to take the long way to Izzy's since the hill was too steep and too wet for the car to climb. As the car struggled up the hill, Oliver hoped against hope that Izzy wasn't home.

CHAPTER TWENTY-NINE

The light on the second floor of Izzy's house had once been a beacon of sorts, calling Oliver back to safety. Now, he subconsciously pleaded for the light to remain extinguished. If he was in luck, Izzy was still sitting at the police station, out of reach of the desperate man with the gun.

Oliver and Anna quietly exited the car, their feet sinking into the soft ground, which quickly turned to mud under the weight of their shoes.

The door sat ajar, and one of the glass panes had been smashed out of it. As Oliver cautiously pushed the door open, he heard rustling from the living room and held his hand out for Anna to wait in the doorway.

Oliver edged into the kitchen, careful to avoid the bad floorboard. Simon was desperately searching for something, and Oliver wasn't eager to confront the armed man, who at this point, had nothing left to lose except for the boy. Oliver heard a sigh of relief and a jingle from the living room.

He was looking for car keys. Surely, Simon can't drive.

If Izzy's keys were at home, so was Izzy—unless Eric had taken her to the station.

Oliver hoped Simon would take the keys and drive off into the night or, hopefully, off the side of a cliff. But instead of running toward the door, Simon flipped the living room lights on.

"Isabelle?" he yelled up the staircase. "Would you take us for a ride? Stay here, boy," he said as he began to climb.

He needs a driver.

The Witch's brother stood in the living room as Simon slowly ascended the steps, gripping his revolver. "I know you're here. Now, come out and say hello."

Oliver pulled the weapon from his belt. It had two barrels, which meant he had precisely two shots to stop Simon. He slowly pulled one of the hammers back, being careful to muffle the click.

As Simon approached the blind corner at the top of the staircase, he let out a sudden yelp and fell backward, toppling down the stairs and onto the living room floor. He lay still for a moment, and the brother stood motionless, with a look of panic on his face.

Izzy descended the staircase, hands wrapped around a wooden baseball bat and ready to swing again. Before she could make it to the bottom, Simon shook himself off and picked up the revolver next to him. Izzy froze as he rose to his feet and pointed the weapon at her.

"How fitting that I should take one last Elder before I depart," he said.

Elder?

"Now, put down the—"

Oliver aimed the bladed pistol as best he could and pulled the trigger. The bullet whizzed past Simon and smashed through the window next to the front door. The shot caught the entire living room by surprise. Simon fell backward against the couch, and while Izzy ducked on the staircase, Simon's son hid behind the coffee table. Anna flew around the corner of the kitchen, brandishing a metal meat tenderizer.

Oliver cocked the second hammer and stepped into the living room as Simon scrambled to his feet and ran toward the door, jerking his son's arm along the way. Oliver held the gun steady, pointing it directly at Simon's back, but couldn't bring himself to fire again.

Simon's footsteps pounded down the front steps as Oliver and Anna ran to the living room to peer out the window. A few moments later, Izzy's car doors slammed shut under the porte cochere, and the engine turned over, revving several times as Simon struggled to shift the car into drive. Oliver stepped out onto the porch just in time to see the car awkwardly peel out from the side of the house and onto the road to town.

Without the Witch, Simon would surely be captured. He was a walking dead man, in more ways than one.

"Call the police, and tell them he's headed toward town!" Oliver shouted through the front door as he ran to the side of the house to grab the police cruiser. He wondered just how far the man would make it without crashing.

He had been correct about the police presence in the town, and only a short time passed before the blare of sirens echoed through the streets. When he reached the square, the tail end of the station wagon appeared in the distance. The vehicle had crashed into the statue of the town founder.

As another cruiser raced toward the square—as fast as a car could race through the narrow streets of Christchurch—Oliver pulled up in the cruiser along the back of the station wagon and ran toward the driver's-side door. Although the wagon had been made of sturdy metal, it was no match for the heavy stone base of the statue, and the front of the car's body had crunched around it, completely collapsing the front bumper and hood. The engine stuttered before dying completely as the officers approached the car.

Simon lay slumped against the steering wheel, blood dripping from his forehead down the cracked leather. Oliver wasn't sure if the injury had come from the impact of the crash or Izzy's baseball bat.

The passenger seat was empty. He craned his head to look for the son but saw no signs of him anywhere. *Did he run? Was he ever in the car to begin with?*

Another cruiser skidded to a halt, and the officers climbed out and moved in. Simon let out a groan and shifted slightly in his seat.

"Back away from the car," one of the officers said from behind. Oliver lifted his palms into the air and slowly backed away. The officer cautiously approached the car and knelt next to Simon once he saw the man was no longer a threat.

Simon was limp as the paramedics lifted him onto the stretcher. After the ambulance carted him away, Oliver was escorted to the police station, sans his obscure pistol. The station was a veritable buzz of activity, and Eric stood in front of an old metal desk, poring over a map of the area, surrounded by several other officers.

The receptionist took one look at Oliver then spun around. "Sir!" she shouted, vying for Eric's attention.

He glanced up from the map. "Thank God," he said under his breath, crossing the room to greet Oliver.

"We got a call from the edge of the woods a little while ago. Something about a commandeered police car hitting a floating woman. What happened out there, and why do you look like you've been playing dress up?"

Oliver ignored the last question. "Simon crossed back into Christchurch and the Wi... woman broke the barrier, so we were able to drive through. She tried to attack the approaching cruiser and—"

Eric held a hand out and stopped Oliver. "Okay, okay. Well, we've got him now. Just have to make sense of whatever happened in the field. We're going to get Izzy and Anna down here too so that we can take statements."

It's over? What about the Witch's brother? Didn't anyone see him?

"I'll call them," Oliver said. "I have to let them know I'm okay."

Eric pointed Oliver toward one of the desk phones in the corner of the room. "You can wait in the interview room once you're done."

Oliver tapped Izzy's number into the dial pad. Anna picked up the phone on the other end. When she heard Oliver's voice, she began to cry.

Oliver spoke quietly, so as not to be overheard by

the others in the station. "Look, they want you and Izzy to come down to the police station. I need you to do something for me, though. Simon's son—the officers in the field must not have seen him. No one besides us knows about him. We have to keep it that way."

"But why would I lie about—"

"He's been locked in that cell for who knows how long. You saw it. If he was smart enough to escape, he'll be smart enough to survive on his own. There's no telling what will happen to him if he's roped into all of this, and he's been through enough. Tell Izzy too." He hung up the receiver and headed toward the interview room.

Oliver sat in the uncomfortable metal chair and waited for his interview. The room was hot, so he took off his heavy overcoat and set it on the interview table. His eye caught the crimson on his cotton shirt. He had completely forgotten about the puncture wound on his left side, and he rolled up his shirt to examine it. Although his skin was stained with clots of dried blood, the wound had completely healed.

CHAPTER THIRTY

The Christchurch paper ran a story about Simon and the Jane Doe who had confronted the police at the edge of the woods, tying them to the town murders and attacks on Madeline and Izzy. After a short stint in the hospital, Simon was taken into police custody and faced charges that would surely put him away for the rest of his life—a life Oliver assumed wouldn't last much longer without his bloody fountain of youth. The lack of a weapon led to obvious questions about why deadly force had been used against the woman, but the dashcam footage put those questions to rest.

The video from the flipped cruiser clearly showed the Witch levitating across the field, and testimony from everyone present that day verified the unbelievable events. Oliver hadn't noticed at the time, but the commandeered cruiser was equipped with a dashcam as well and had managed to capture several glimpses of the town on the other side of the patch when Oliver crossed into Briarwood, with Anna and Simon, through the crack in the portal.

Finally, he had cold, hard evidence the Witch and Briarwood were both real. But as the people of Christchurch had done hundreds of years before, they chose to bury the truth with silence and quaint village delusions. The paper made no mention of the more whimsical details of Simon's siege on Christchurch, and the dashcam footage only made it to a select few. Although no one spoke of the Witch or Simon, in public at least, none of the townspeople were daring enough to approach the briar patch after that day.

Oliver was sweeping debris into a neat pile. Several large mounds speckled Izzy's living room floor, and Pan had made it his job to run through each of them, causing such a mess that Izzy had to confine him to the bedroom. Although Izzy's life leading up to the murders had been one of a pariah's, she had found a new level of acceptance among the townspeople— Madeline made sure of it. A crew of helpers had arrived to assist her, Oliver, and Anna in cleaning up the mess from the attacks. The support was sorely needed since most of her belongings, on the first floor at least, had been left in complete shambles. Izzy's furniture had been broken and splintered, and several of her sculptures had been shattered across the floor. Oliver noticed her wiping a tear from the corner of her eye every now and then, but he was certain the resilient woman would be able to quickly fill the room once again with a new batch of eclectic odds and ends.

"You never told me you were an Elder," he blurted out as he helped her collect the pieces of an abstract plaster bust.

"Excuse me?" she replied.

"Simon. It was one of the last things he said—something about taking care of one more Elder."

Izzy blushed.

"That's why Madeline took everything so personally. You weren't just helping around town—you were an Elder."

"Well, it certainly didn't last for long," Izzy replied. "We were at each other's throats by the end of the year. I was unceremoniously discharged."

Anna had busied herself in the kitchen, pulling the knives out of the wooden doorframe and putting all the drawers and cabinets back into proper order.

After several days of cleanup, the house was finally completely cleared of debris. Oliver was sitting at the kitchen table with Izzy and Anna. A thought had been building in the back of his mind.

"I have to go back to the city," he said out of nowhere, looking into his swirling Irish coffee.

The pronouncement seemed to catch the other two by surprise.

"What? Why?" Anna asked.

"I just think it's time to go back. My apartment is just sitting there, and I won't be able to pay the rent much longer without some kind of income."

Oliver had never planned to stay forever. Christchurch was intended to be a momentary reprieve from his life in the city. The time had come to grow up and go back to face real life once again. Whatever *real life* meant, he wasn't quite sure.

Izzy didn't say anything at first but just sat and stirred her coffee.

"I've been thinking," she said after an extended silence, "we could use some permanent help around here. I'm not as spry as I used to be. Hopefully, Anna will take over the bakery when it's time, but she's going to need help, and we've got the bees to take care of. I'd be able to pay you."

"I really do appreciate the offer, but my life's been on pause long enough, and it's time that I do something about it."

Izzy seemed wounded by his words. "You have been doing something about it. Your life isn't on pause.

This is it. What you were doing back in the city—that's what you should be running away from."

Later that night, Oliver sat on Izzy's porch and looked down at the tree line across the field. The town of Briarwood sat locked away behind the patch, behind the invisible wall that obscured it from view. He wondered if he'd ever make it back and what would happen to Gideon, now that Mercy had likely succumbed to her wounds. He felt guilty for leaving them behind after they'd helped him so much.

And what about Simon's son? Oliver empathized with him. *Where is he going to go? And who ended up with the coin?*

Oliver stared at a blank page of his yellow legal pad. His resume was in sore need of updating, and he wondered how he would talk about his previous position. *Surely, they'll want to call my old boss for a reference, right? Maybe I'll just take it off, say I took a gap year—more like two years at this point.* Without the job with Mr. Sally, his resume would look the same as it had when he had walked across the aisle at graduation. He sketched out a list of new skills:

- Beekeeping and Honey Harvesting
- Baking and Bakery Management
- Custom Car Painting
- Murder Solving
- Witch Hunting

The list quickly devolved into absurdity before he scratched it out completely.

CHAPTER THIRTY-ONE

Oliver stood in the doorway of his studio apartment, clutching two paper grocery bags. The light from the dreary sky cast a gray filter over his possessions enclosed by the whitewashed walls he had longed to forget.

After setting the bags on the table, Oliver stepped over to the window overlooking the city. He'd spent too much time in this apartment, too far removed from the people below him.

"Where should we start?" Anna asked from behind. She cradled a stack of flattened cardboard boxes under each arm.

"If you two want to start in the kitchen, I'll start packing up my clothes," he replied, pulling the cleaning supplies out of the grocery bags.

Izzy rounded the corner and came into the apartment. "You mean to tell me that you had to climb that staircase every—oh, how wonderful!" She had been distracted by the large cast of characters adorning the apartment walls. "Did you do all of these?"

"Every one," he replied.

"We have to take these with us. We should hang them in the bakery!"

Oliver laughed as he pulled a box from the pile and began to tape it together.

The studio apartment left little room for storage, so the trio had finished packing and cleaning within a few hours. Oliver took one last look at the empty room. Within a short amount of time, all evidence of his existence had been completely wiped away. Soon, someone else would live here, and Oliver would be long forgotten. The more he thought about it, though, it wasn't the fault of the city or his old job, for that matter. He'd chosen this place, to live in isolation. Despite the drama of living in Christchurch, Izzy and Anna had become family like he'd never known before. In his own strange way, he had become part of the fabric of the town, made connections, and found a pair of people who had brought something out in him he didn't even know existed.

Oliver dropped his apartment keys into the landlord's mailbox and carried the last of the boxes to the car. They'd managed to fit nearly everything, except for the old desk that sat under Oliver's window.

Izzy had come dangerously close to purchasing an ordinary white delivery van after her station wagon had been totaled but couldn't bring herself to do it. Fortunately, Oliver noticed a for-sale ad in the paper a few days after the incident. The cream-colored station wagon was a different model and year from Izzy's, but she fell in love when she saw the wood paneling and tail fins.

As Izzy pulled the car out of its parking spot, Oliver kept a close eye on the twin bed strapped to the roof.

"Oh, would you relax," Anna said. "The straps are tight. It's not going anywhere."

Oliver watched his old haunts fly by as they headed toward the highway. This journey to Christchurch was different than the last, and as the day progressed, he felt a weight gradually lifting from atop his shoulders. He still had reality to deal with and hadn't even told his mother about the move out of the city. That conversation would certainly end in a fight. But for now, he felt an overwhelming sense of freedom. Although the future was more unclear than ever before, he saw great potential in the unknown.

ENJOY THE BOOK?

Continue Oliver's Journey with Book 2

Oliver Crum and The Grim Menagerie

Check Out Chris Cooper's First Book

The Dreadful Objects

Leave a Review

Reviews help tremendously. Please consider leaving a review on Amazon or Goodreads!

Find an Error?

Loved the book but found an error? Let us know at Dreadfulmedia.com.

ABOUT THE AUTHOR

Chris Cooper is a writer, college professor, novice coffee roaster, and recovering engineer. He lived and worked in Japan, where he developed an obscure obsession for fancy fountain pens and currently lives in Ohio with his partner and Australian Cattle Terrier. Both enjoy going for walks. Chris writes supernatural thrillers full of colorful three-dimensional characters, macabre adventures, and twisty turny plots.

www.ingramcontent.com/pod-product-compliance
Lightning Source LLC
Chambersburg PA
CBHW071543110726
47908CB00007B/1977